The Cure

Jonathan Bate is well known as a reviewer and essayist and is the author of several works of non-fiction, including *The Genius of Shakespeare*, published by Picador. *The Cure for Love* is his first novel.

Jonathan Bate

The Cure for Love

PICADOR

for Paula

First published 1998 by Picador

This edition published 1999 by Picador
an imprint of Macmillan Publishers Ltd
25 Eccleston Place, London SW1W 9NF
Basingstoke and Oxford

Associated companies throughout the world

ISBN 0 330 34732 2

3 5 7 9 8 6 4 2

A CIP catalogue record for this book is available from
the British Library.

Typeset by SetSystems Ltd, Saffron Walden, Essex
Printed and bound in Great Britain by
Mackays of Chatham plc, Chatham, Kent

I

Conversations

1

It was her rule never to speak first.

At the beginning there would be a few formalities. Then she would let silence fill the room. She did not like it in summer when the gardeners were mowing outside. Snowy days were best.

From the point of view of whoever was on the couch or in the chair – that was one of the formalities: 'You may choose' – it would seem like five minutes, ten, of deep embarrassment. She knew that it was rarely more than two or three. Then, without thinking, they would say whatever happened to be in their head at the moment when they could no longer stand the silence. They would never say what was really on their mind.

'My first memory was of having no memory.'

It was another of her rules never to respond to what they said first. The second silence was always briefer than the first.

She watched and waited. He was pale, angular. He sat uneasily, half on and half off the chair, with his legs tucked underneath, his hands folded listlessly on his knees, his head bowed. One of his elbows was leaning – not resting, it seemed to her – on the arm of the chair, as if in fear of its having no right to be there.

'I knew where I was, but had no idea who I was.'

Now was the moment to press a little: 'What do you mean by "who I was"?'

She watched him shift in the chair. She had made him think. This was always among the first indications of the kind of encounter it was going to be. Was he used to reflecting upon himself? Did the act of doing so make him confused, uncomfortable, hostile? Would her task be to pierce through the intellect to the emotions, or would it be to pick up fragments of pain and piece them into a story that could be lived with?

'Looking at myself in the mirror, I knew that I was myself: I had no doubt that these were the features with which I had always lived. But what *always* might mean, what it would be to *have lived* rather than to live, I knew not.'

This was unusual. The sentences were formed like written thoughts. She needed a moment to ensure that she remained ahead of him.

'Let's start at the beginning,' she said, 'and let's keep it as simple as we can for the moment.'

'I had been found without a coat. The fever – pneumonia? – had been their first concern. I had suffered from delirium. I had talked and talked in my half-consciousness. Cogent sentences, but to weirdly varied purposes. And, they said, in a strangely florid style. Like someone in an old book. But you know all this – the other hospital must have given you a file. Why are you asking me what you already know?'

She knew that he had been found without a coat, without identification. Wallet, driving licence: they must have been in the pocket of the jacket he was not wearing. An early-morning fisherman had stumbled upon him, miles from anywhere, at the foot of a steep rocky bank. Had he fallen or had he thrown himself? And what was this Englishman, obviously no vagrant, doing without a coat deep in the Scottish countryside before dawn?

The usual pattern with head injuries was that there would be a period of confusion, its length dependent on the severity of the blow and the duration of unconsciousness, but that long-term memory would soon return. The memory of the blow itself and the time immediately leading up to it would perhaps come later, though often it did not come back at all.

This case, however, had been complicated by the influenza symptoms. The fever had aggravated the post-traumatic confusional state. The process of establishing whether there was any lasting brain damage could only begin after three days, when his temperature had subsided and his hallucinations ceased.

When questioned, her notes told her, he became irritable. One kind of question he could answer with ease: how many fingers am I holding up, what was the name of the Princess of Wales. It was the other kind that stressed him: what is your name, what is your age, where were you born, what is your occupation.

Another of her rules: don't answer their questions too soon or too directly. Don't let them try to set the agenda. So she did not tell him why she was asking what she already knew. Instead, she met his question with a question. This was one of the things she liked about the job: its resemblance to a Socratic symposium. Or a chess match.

'What happens when people ask you questions about yourself?'

She detected a slight dilation of his pupils. Anger and

5

panic in equal proportions. She reckoned that he was not the sort to close himself down – her instincts were already telling her that he would be a rewarding patient. Still, her guess was that to begin with he would neither go with the anger nor reveal the panic.

'A black tunnel,' he said.

The panic, but a very encouraging willingness to acknowledge it.

Silence. She did not want to say 'Go on'; she knew that she could suggest to him without speaking that she wanted him to do so. She looked him in the eye.

On a reflex, his head turned. His eyes were everywhere in the room save upon hers. He was talking so as to avoid contact.

'When I searched for answers to all their questions, I entered a black tunnel. There was no means of orientation, no path to light at the other end. The only escape was to turn back to the entrance through which they had sent me. To say, O, I don't know, no, yes; to say, I don't know, I'm sorry, I don't know, I can't see anything, I don't know, nothing, I don't know, there is no answer.'

Then he was staring at her, but blankly. Staring through her, the dilation extreme. She let a moment pass. There was a gust of wind outside and her eye followed his through the window and settled on a tumbling leaf. She remembered an autumn walk with her first boyfriend. 'Concentrate, Foster,' she said to herself. He was calmer now.

'But then an answer came?'

'Yes. I knew when it was day and when it was night, but I could not be sure how many days passed. Then a new patient appeared in the next bed. The previous one had complained about my night ravings – though I was told these were becoming less frequent and less prolonged – whereas the older man who replaced him took what seemed to be a genial interest in me. A vein stood out on the eggshell of his forehead. In the morning he said to the nurse: "I think he might be called William something – or someone very close to him is a William. It's a name he keeps coming back to in his sleep." My first instinct was denial. I did not know what I was called, but I was certain it wasn't William. Then I thought some more and, though my head ached when I forced it back there, I went into the tunnel and on taking a few steps in the darkness I was suddenly conscious of the tiniest pinprick of light ahead of me.'

He paused, reliving the dawn.

She had her confirmation of the diagnosis made by the head-injury unit. She was back in a chilly lecture room, taking notes. 'Amnesiacs forget the incidents of their daily life as fast as they occur.' Post-traumatic amnesia rarely involved extended *retrograde* (she had underlined the word) memory loss; the defining symptom was *anterograde* loss – difficulty in retaining new impressions, things subsequent to the onset of the amnesiac state. Had his amnesia still been post-traumatic, he would not have remembered what had happened a mere two minutes ago, certainly not this incident in the clinical ward two weeks ago. The strong inference had to be that his underlying condition was psychogenic, not organic.

She remembered something else from the lecture on amnesia. 'Malingering can never be ruled out.' She had hated the word. When writing up her notes, she had added a growl in neat square brackets: 'Malingering [grr!] can never be ruled out.' The accusation smacked of everything she loathed about the medical profession's semi-disbelief in mental illness. It was bad enough that half the patients did not believe that their illness had anything to do with the mind – 'Why is it that I just can't stop crying all the time? It must be some allergy, don't you think, doctor?' – but they had the excuse that such disbelief was a defence. What infuriated her was the profession's scepticism. 'Malingering.'

The main task in this first session was to win his trust, make sure he didn't get the idea that she might regard him as a malingerer.

Time to break his reverie: 'And then?'

'Yes – and then I said, "Yes, my name is William." I had perhaps hoped that saying it would convince me of its truth, but I remained far from sure. Still, it was enough for them. There had been a question mark at the head of the chart at the foot of my bed. When I returned from the bathroom that morning it had been changed to *William ?*.'

This time he stopped abruptly, whereas previously he had trailed off. Usually, this meant that something was being hidden. Without knowing why, she felt like taking a risk and pushing at it.

'Did your concerned neighbour tell you anything else about your night ravings, as you call them?'

He looked startled. She knew what that meant: he was thinking, She knows there's something else. In this circumstance, she could usually predict whether or not a patient would respond with denial. This time, she wasn't sure. He was her first amnesiac.

For the first time, he was the one to initiate direct eye contact: 'Yes, as a matter of fact he did.' Then silence.

The chess match had begun in earnest. He had decided that she was going to have to work for the information she wanted. For now, she would have to let him suppose that he was dictating terms. She was confident that she saw many moves further ahead than he could have done.

'You don't have to share it with me if you don't want to.'

'Why wouldn't I want to?'

'That was the impression you gave.'

'I've got nothing to hide. I mean, for god's sake, I thought the whole reason I'm here is to find out things about me, not cover them up.'

She drew the passion from the outburst, pleased to have provoked it. Then slowed the tempo: 'Of course it is, William, but we need to find them out slowly, in the right order. You've taken a battering and it'll be best not to try to do too much too soon.'

'So you assume my name is William.'

'I don't assume anything, but you gave the impression that you were happy to live with the name. Or is there something else you'd rather I call you?'

'Content to live with it, not happy. So what should I call you?'

'What would you be most comfortable calling me?'

'I'd be most comfortable if you stopped answering questions with questions.'

Let it pass, she thought. Work for the trust: 'You can call me either Mrs Foster or Laura, whichever you prefer.'

She had written her thesis under the name Laura Foster

9

and wanted that always to be her professional name. When she married, she found that it made most patients more comfortable to call her Mrs, so although she was legally Mrs Sellinger, she practised as Mrs Foster. There was no reason to revert to Ms now that she was divorced.

'Shouldn't you be *Doctor* Foster?' Then he smiled for the first time. 'Wasn't he in a Beatrix Potter story – went to Gloucester, didn't he?'

She smiled back. 'A nursery rhyme, actually. So you do remember something that you read as a child. That's encouraging, isn't it? The notes on your referral papers said that you were especially upset about not remembering things from books.'

She was pleased with this turn. The lightening of tone had helped to build the trust; the introduction of childhood was always a moment she relished. And there would be no need to explain the reasons why her doctorate was not formally recognized in her official title in the hospital.

'I'll call you Laura, if it's all the same to you.'

'Good.' This time they smiled in unison rather than succession.

She had learned to read the atmosphere in her little room. She knew that now she could ask him directly about the other thing the man in the next bed had said.

He got there before she did: 'While I was inspecting the temperature chart with my name added to it, my concerned neighbour said quietly, "There was something else."'

He paused, pulling back from the revelation.

'Take your time, William.'

Then it was as if he were composing himself to tell a story. 'I looked at him vacantly. "Come here," he said in a conspiratorial voice. Then he said, "I wasn't going to tell the nurse because it's probably a private affair, if you know what I mean." Seedy emphasis on that last phrase, you know?'

Laura nodded and let William continue.

'So he pauses for dramatic effect. Then he hits me with it: "William wasn't the only name you kept repeating." He pauses again, stretching it out. Of course I should have known what was coming. "There was also a woman." Third pause. A real melodramatist, isn't he? Then, what do they call it, a double whammy? "Well, in fact *two* women's names," says Mister Know-it-all. "Though very similar to each other," he teases.'

'You're right to be angry about his way of carrying on,' interjected Laura. But William was not listening.

'His fourth pause irritated me intensely. I could tell that he was enjoying keeping me in suspense. I did not break his *expectant silence*. "Don't you want to know them, then?" he asks. I would have liked to reply, No, but you obviously want to tell me. All I managed was, "I'm tired."'

He faltered, as if the tiredness were returning. Laura offered sympathy. She did not push him to the next detail. He would provide it when he was ready. This was a lucky break: since the man with the eggshell head was the enemy, William was casting her as his friend.

'So then he said, "Sometimes it was Sarah and sometimes it was Sally." The names didn't mean anything to me. I just replied in a neutral voice that I had a headache and needed to sleep some more. But he was determined to get the last word. "Just one other thing," he adds. "There was also a strange phrase you kept repeating."'

Laura said nothing.

'He wasn't going to let me rest until he had divulged it. I concede him a weary, Yes? He comes back with, "The seven-inch conversation." I echo the words inanely: "The seven-inch conversation?" "Yes," – the smug bastard – "very curious, wouldn't you say?" Without replying, I got back into bed. Angry with myself for initially misreading his intrusiveness as concern, I closed my eyes. What business did he have to make innuendo out of my delirium? I determined to do all I could to stop talking in my sleep or semi-consciousness. I didn't want others knowing who I was before I knew myself.'

Whatever state it had been spoken in, the phrase was so comically Freudian that she had to work to keep a straight face. Such moments were an occupational hazard. She had developed a way of bending the little finger of her left hand and pricking her palm with her long nail in order to stop herself laughing. Then at the weekend, on the phone to her sister, she would dissolve into giggles.

Discussion of the seven-inch conversation could come later. For now, it was his overall performance that interested her. He remembered the exchange with the eggshell man in such detail, right down to the length of the pauses between exchanges and the tone of voice in each remark. His anger suggested a deep emotional investment, yet his own tone in telling the story had been strangely neutral. His voice had not altered even on the 'smug bastard' interjection. It was almost as if he had been telling someone else's story, not his own.

He needed to be congratulated for opening up: 'You

seem relieved to have told me this, William. Is it the first time you've talked about it?'

'Of course it is, those other doctors were only interested in whether I knew what time of day it was. They said that with a couple of weeks' relaxation my memory would come back – they weren't interested in helping me find it.'

'It's for that help you've come here, William. That's why you were transferred. Once they'd done all the scans and established that there was no damage to your brain, there was no point in keeping you in the head-injury unit. Now tell me, are you settling in here reasonably well?'

She did not want to do any more work this first session. Her next line of questioning was obvious – to unlock some more about Sarah or Sally. But if this woman or these women had been the ultimate cause of his fall, they would have to be approached slowly, or his defences would become impenetrable. A very delicate manoeuvre would be required. His current extremity of retrograde amnesia meant that he was not aware of the traumatic significance of S. But as soon as he became aware, he would be likely to block the knowledge a second time. Her task was to draw the significance from him before he discovered it himself, and thus be in a position to help him overcome it. Looked at like this, the process was the same as in a classic psychoanalysis.

The problem was time. As far as the hospital was concerned, her sole task was to establish the man's identity so that he could be discharged. But her instincts told her that too quick a discharge would be unproductive, potentially catastrophic. If his fall had been a suicide attempt, what was to stop him trying again? She shivered, remembering Nicholas Freeman, with his glassy blue eyes. A boy of seventeen, only her second patient, whom she had been forced to let go too soon.

She had called her sister on hearing the news. 'Amanda, that boy Nick I was telling you about . . .'

Amanda had been prepared. She had known something was wrong. In the course of several long phone calls, she had persuaded Laura that she must go on, that there were bound to be tragedies and setbacks, but that her life's work would be to save others before they reached the brink. 'Courage, sister,' she had said.

Laura had suppressed the nagging suspicion that the very act of dredging up long-buried trauma had driven the Freeman boy to his end. She had got on with the treatment of her other patients. She had begun to win the respect even of those doctors who were sceptical of therapy and who set store by drugs alone. But still whenever a tricky discharge was discussed at the weekly team meeting she would ask, 'Can we be sure they won't attempt to take their own life?'

In the case of 'William', she was already fairly sure that his fall had not been wilful. Even through the amnesia, she could discern an inner fortitude about him. She read endurance, not abandonment, in his care for language and the precision of his memory. How could an amnesiac have such powers of recall? Was he faking his memory loss? If so, then why? Those were the really interesting questions.

She caught herself. This was her professional weakness: to regard certain cases as *interesting*, not to restrict herself to the business of the cure. If cure there could be.

No suicide risk, then, but she wouldn't say so at the team

meeting on Monday. It was a card she could play if premature discharge began to look likely. For now, she would diagnose total retrograde amnesia, a blow to the head being the proximate cause, but with severe psychogenic aggravation. She would propose three sessions per week, and in order to speed the process – 'I know the pressure we have on places' – would devise some form of additional supporting therapy.

While she was following this line of thought, William had been saying that he was not exactly settling in, since a ward full of depressives and headcases was hardly the kind of place where you could settle. But he supposed he had to accept that memory loss was a mental problem, so he was a headcase himself.

'Just remember I'm not one of your regular patients,' he said, cockily more than defensively. 'I don't need a shrink, I just need someone with expertise in amnesia.'

He then asked her if she had worked with his kind of patient before. She reassured him that his was a textbook case. All they needed was time. Then she dismissed him.

'That will be all for now, William. This was really just a preliminary meeting to see where we are and for the two of us to begin to get to know each other. I'll be suggesting that we see each other on Mondays, Wednesdays and Fridays. Over the weekend, I just want you to relax and find your feet. You'll be glad not to be in a clinical ward any more. You can walk in the grounds here, read in the library and so on. And can you do something for me? If any memories do come back, make sure you clock them. Every little thing helps, and on Monday we'll be able to talk about whatever you come up with.'

2

Laura was convinced that therapy could only work if there was emotional involvement on both sides.

She argued endlessly with Amanda about this. Amanda was a lecturer. She regarded the teacher–pupil relationship in her profession as no different from the therapist–patient bond in Laura's. Of course a pupil must be given attention and encouragement, she would say. Sometimes it could even be helpful to allow them the illusion that you *really* cared about them, like a child or a lover. But that must always be an absolute illusion. The moment you really did start caring you should get out. Professional distance was all.

Laura disagreed. 'But you teach literature – words and emotions. How can you be so cold about it?'

'I'm not cold about the literature, I'm cool with the students.'

'There's something dangerous and dishonest about that, Amanda. You're just sublimating. The real emotion is there in the classroom, but you try to bottle it up in the imaginary emotion of the books you talk about. One day the cork will blow off.'

Amanda's response was always the same. She would explain that Laura was merely reiterating Plato's argument against the poets. He had said that they stir up unhealthily strong emotions and therefore they were dangerous and should be banished from the republic. But Aristotle had the answer to Plato. His theory of catharsis: by stirring up the unhealthy emotions in the artificial space of the theatre, you could purge them out of your system without doing any real harm.

Laura found it hard to argue with this, since she had a lot of faith – too much, her more conservative colleagues often said – in *acting out* and even in drama therapy. Sometimes she thought that she should devote herself exclusively to group work.

Instead of entering the argument intellectually, she would point out that Amanda was talking about ordinary kids, whereas she worked with extreme cases. And with them the gut instinct was always right: they needed real care, they would see through any kind of insincerity. They needed love.

Besides, she said on other occasions, Freud knew all about catharsis too. It was the very basis of his method. He had discovered that the recall of forgotten memories was only effective as a cure if it was accompanied by a release of the associated – hitherto repressed – emotions. The release meant that the therapy room was an emotionally charged environment. But, in the hands of the skilled therapist, a controlled one.

Laura had a way of clearing confusion from her mind and focusing herself. She used it when patients threw out so much material that she could not think which line to follow; she also used it in arguments with Amanda. She would stop trying to weigh up every possibility. Instead she would say to herself, 'What's the paradigm?' Sometimes it would be a phrase ('Amnesiacs forget the incidents of their daily life as fast as they occur'), sometimes a case history.

In answer to Amanda's arguments against emotional involvement, the paradigm was a case she had read about. A patient spent seventeen years in psychoanalysis with first one, then another, highly reputable analyst. During that time he did not ever experience a single emotion of even the slightest intensity. Then he moved to a therapist who allowed acting out. One day he and his new therapist had a real fight. He felt liberated. He announced that he needed no more therapy. According to available information three years later, the cure was complete.

But she could not deny that her brief marriage was a casualty of the emotional investment necessary for effective therapy. Day after day at work, she received pain into herself and gave back comfort to her patients. When she went home in the evenings, all she wanted was to unwind. To anaesthetize herself with a glass of wine in the bath as soon as she got in, with another over a light meal, and with brandy and television before bed. Simple cooking was her salvation; its results could be tasted within minutes, whereas those of therapy were invisible for months or years. A student friendship had taken her one summer to the Chinese quarter of San Francisco, where she had learnt the art made possible by the wok – a limited repertoire of basic ingredients rendered infinitely variable, perpetually appetizing, through different combinations of spice.

Emotionally, there was nothing left to give to Jack.

It had worked before they were married. A brief daily phone call after supper, but otherwise no contact from Mondays to Thursdays. Then on Friday nights, dinner or a movie, and love making. The week's work forgotten. On Saturdays they would go to a gallery or walk in the country. The sex was satisfying. Then indolence, coffee and the Sunday newspapers. High tea (Jack's nomenclature) together, then home to phone Amanda and prepare for the morning.

Why had she let it change? She had taken Jack's ultimatum too seriously. All or nothing, he had said. He had turned thirty, he wanted to settle, she must marry him or they must part. To begin with, he showed understanding, gave her space on weekday evenings. He took himself off to the gym. Sundays became the flashpoint: if he wasn't going to be allowed to spend time with his own wife four evenings a week, he was damn well having her full attention for the whole weekend. She had accepted the compromise for a time, but with her new job at the hospital it became impossible. The team meeting took place every Monday morning at half past eight, and she had to be absolutely on top of her material. Sunday nights were given back to preparation.

Now that Jack was gone, she treated Friday as any other weekday, often making a point of staying late in her office and catching up on admin. She kept her Sunday routine. Instead of exchanging titbits from the papers with Jack, she did so over the phone with Amanda. Saturdays were the only lonely day.

The Sunday phone conversation with Amanda was sacrosanct. From national news they would turn to their own respective weeks. Amanda would sound off about her male colleagues, then launch into a vertiginous account of the latest development of her research. She was turning her doctoral thesis into a book about the influence on Henry

James's novels of the philosophical and psychological theories of his brother William James. She was going to argue that, paradoxically, William was the better storyteller, Henry the better philosopher and psychologist.

Laura liked to bounce ideas off her sister. They always had similar intuitions, but Amanda was better at rationalizing them. Laura often spoke about her patients, though only ever using their Christian names and never saying anything specific about their background.

She had been preparing her initial assessment of 'William' for the Monday morning team meeting. All the notes from her training were carefully filed. There had been no difficulty in finding a paradigm for classic post-traumatic amnesia.

A golf club greenkeeper had been thrown from his motorcycle. There was a bruise in the left frontal region and slight bleeding from the left ear, but the X-ray revealed no fracture. Recovery of consciousness was slow, but after a week he was able to converse sensibly, and all his functions were normal. However, he remembered nothing about his identity or his past. Then his childhood came back to him. After another two weeks he remembered a period of five years he had spent in Australia as a young man. But the two years preceding the accident remained a complete blank. Six weeks after the injury he returned to the village where he had been working for those two years. Everything looked strange and he had no recollection of ever having been there before. He lost his way on more than one occasion. Still feeling a stranger, he returned to work; he was able to perform his tasks satisfactorily, but had difficulty in remembering what he had actually done during the day. Then, within about ten weeks, the events of the past two years were gradually recollected and finally he was able to remember everything up to within a few minutes of the accident.

This did not fit William's case. He had no difficulty in remembering what he had done during the days since his return to consciousness. He had an uncannily full recollection of the nosy man with the eggshell head. The tests and scans had been conclusive: his brain was functioning normally. It followed that there must be an hysterical factor.

She knew what Bill Braddock would say in the team meeting: give him an intravenous injection of sodium pentothal, let it take hold, then order him to rouse himself, push him hard to recount everything he remembered of his accident and what led up to it, and, hey presto, all would be revealed. She would let BB have his say, confident that Andrews, the team leader, would respect her own methods.

Barbiturate hypnosis was double anathema to her. Drugs were not the answer. As for hypnosis, Freud and Breuer had begun by using it to gain access to the past, but Freud had then abandoned it in favour of free verbal association. Psychoanalysis had been invented as a substitute for hypnosis. One must never revert to it. The hypnotist had absolute power of suggestion, his technique was open to the most terrible abuses. Therapy depended on emotion going two ways. The therapist had to make herself vulnerable.

Sometimes, though, she wondered whether there really was such a difference. Especially when the patient had chosen the couch rather than the chair. When their eyes were closed, in the moments of concentrated silence, they might just as well have been hypnotized. The subject relinquishes the gaze and relies on the voice. However hard she might try not to put ideas into their heads, she knew that she always did.

Another memory-committed phrase came to her: 'Hypnosis short-circuits the resistances.' Hypnosis within psychotherapy was generally regarded as heretical. But so too was acting out. Laura liked to think of herself as a bit of a heretic, a risk-taker. Her best results came when she trusted herself to throw away the rule book. Yes, she could kick-start 'The Case of *William* ?' by means of hypnosis.

She remembered another case she had read up on. A patient had 'forgotten' the last twelve years of her life. It had been in France in the days when abortion was illegal. The woman had assisted at an abortion, been reported and convicted, but finally pardoned. She had become depressed, then suddenly she had forgotten everything. The abortion was symbolic for her of her unhappy marriage; the amnesia extended back twelve years because that had been the length of the marriage. All that was required to recover her memory was a single hypnotic session during which she was asked to give an account of the 'forgotten' data and told that she would be able to remember everything on awakening.

The telephone rang. Amanda.

They laughed about the seven-inch conversation. Amanda quoted her favourite saying of Freud: 'You know, a cigar can also be a cigar.'

When Laura told her sister about the condition in which William had been found, Amanda said, 'That's seriously weird.'

Laura knew what this heralded. Amanda was only a year older than her; always close to each other, they had the telepathy of twins. And, as with twins, there were frequent little coincidences which made their lives seem to run on parallel tracks.

That very week, Amanda had read in William James the story of the Reverend Ansel Bourne.

One day the Reverend Bourne withdrew five hundred and fifty-one dollars from his bank in Providence, Rhode Island. He paid his bills and got into a Pawtucket horse-car. Nothing was heard of him for two months. He was reported missing, presumed murdered. Meanwhile a man calling himself A. J. Brown rented a shop in Norristown, Pennsylvania, stocking it with stationery, confectionery, fruit and small articles. Six weeks later A. J. Brown woke up in a fright and asked where he was. He said that his name was Ansel Bourne and that he was entirely ignorant of Norristown, knew nothing about shopkeeping. The last thing he remembered – it seemed only yesterday – was drawing the money from the bank in Providence. He was at first assumed to be insane, but a telegram to his nephew revealed that he was telling the truth. He was taken home. He had lost twenty pounds in weight and had conceived such a horror of the idea of the candy store that he vowed never to set foot in one again.

Laura remembered now. The condition was called the fugue. A person simply gets up and walks away. They can be gone for hours, days, even weeks.

'Was that the end of the story?' she asked her sister. Amanda was explaining that what had interested her were the details – the candy, the five hundred and fifty-one dollars and the Pawtucket horse-car (though she did not yet know precisely what that was). They supported her thesis that William James was really the storyteller, Henry the psychologist.

'Yes, except that under hypnosis, Bourne told of his peregrinations during the lost fortnight, and all the details were subsequently corroborated. Brother William was very interested in hypnosis, you know.'

3

The go-ahead had been given for three times a week, but the need for a speedy resolution had been stressed. Her nine-thirty slot on Mondays, Wednesdays and Fridays was vacant, so she went straight from the team meeting into the first proper session with William. She had decided to begin with one or two orthodox encounters, then go for hypnosis if no progress had been made.

She spent the first half-hour building confidence, easing relaxation. Asked him about his weekend, told him a little about the work of the hospital, the range of patients. Let him ask a few questions about her, enough to make her a human being, a partner in conversation rather than a shaman.

She wanted him to have the assurance that she did not consider herself his 'shrink'. Her opportunity came when he challenged her about his symptoms. The trick would be to let him suppose that she ascribed his memory loss solely to the accident.

She explained about post-traumatic amnesia. That in such cases there was no permanent damage to the brain and there would be a full recovery of what had been lost. He had already come out of the post-traumatic phase, as strictly defined, in which consciousness was absent or only partial. But with blows to the head as severe as his must have been, there was often a period in which there was difficulty in

25

either processing new information or recovering old. His response to questions suggested that although his store of general knowledge was fully intact, he had completely lost all personal memory. To piece together all of his identity would be a slow process, perhaps a matter of weeks or even months. The recovery would be patchy, fragmentary, unpredictable. There would be islands of clarity in a sea of oblivion.

She explained how there might be an oscillation between recent and distant memory, but that insofar as there was a pattern in such cases the tendency was to begin with the distant past and to begin with spots or moments. As time went on, the memories would become more sustained, more connected. Those of adult life would have a more fleshed-out narrative.

The reconstruction, she assured him, would gradually approach the time when the traumatic event took place, but the last few moments before the shock itself would probably never be known.

'But you mustn't worry,' she said. 'Everything else *will* come back. It takes a lot to dislodge the memory altogether. Organically speaking, it's the most enduring part of us with the possible exception of scar tissue.'

He thought for a moment and then looked her in the eyes: 'You mean that memory is mental scar tissue?'

She did not reply. She was thinking that such an attitude to memory confirmed her diagnosis that his 'forgetting' was an act of repression. She was feeling sad.

She left spaces of silence. She began to feel confident that she was in control of the rhythm of things. When she slowed her breathing, he spoke more slowly.

Then she was ready.

'So did you come up with anything over the weekend?'

He told her that something had happened in the day room on Sunday afternoon. He described the incident slowly, deliberately, with quirky details. Almost as if he were telling a story, not relating the events of the previous day.

It had been drizzly. He had noted that the word the nurses used was unfamiliar: 'dreak'? His ignorance of the dialect had led him to wonder what he had been doing in Scotland. It made him realize that he couldn't have been in the country for long. His accent had intimated to the first doctors that he was not Scots, but they had assumed he was living there, perhaps in Edinburgh. He was sure now that this was wrong. But hard as he tried to think, he could come up with no reason why he had been found in Scotland when he lived, he was sure, in England. Then the incident:

'Someone had hung a damp sweater over the back of a chair close to the gas fire. Something in the musty smell of drying clothes sent me back into the tunnel. For the first time I had some confidence that the light ahead of me would be there – and that it would be a little brighter than it had been when the name of William pricked it into view.'

Laura inclined a little, as a way of showing him that he had her full attention.

'Suddenly there was the sound of a boy's and a girl's voice. Probably bored by their visit to an elderly relative recovering from a *funny turn*. They chased each other into the day room. The chair with the sweater over its back was falling towards the fire.'

He looked away. She gave him time.

He did not continue, so she helped: 'It's often the way that nothing happens when you *try* to remember, but that a chance happening, even a smell, can unlock something.' She recalled her own thrill of recognition upon reading in a textbook that smell was the first of our senses, that the cerebral hemispheres themselves were originally offshoots from the olfactory stalk.

He wasn't listening. His eyes seemed glazed.

Then his voice altered, itself became glazed, like the voice of a sleep-talker. Laura was mesmerized.

'The child put his hand into the flame. He had always been drawn to the fire, not only because it was the place of warmth in the stone house but also because it seemed to be the centre of the home. His father sitting by it reading. His sister standing over it warming herself. His brother lying on the floor sketching. His mother bringing in the scuttle, sighing because of the weight. He often knelt in front of it and looked into the glowing coals. He imagined taking one between his fingers. In the scuttle they were black, on the fire they were red, when his mother cleared them before beginning the fire again they were grey. So if he took one between his fingers and removed it from the fire would it instantly turn grey? Or would it fade slowly? And if he blew upon it, as his father sometimes pumped the bellows when impatient for a taller flame, would it return to red?'

She did not want to interrupt; she wished she had a tape recorder.

'He wanted to experiment, to find the moment at which the coal faded. He wanted the power for himself: to choose the moment when the fading coal awoke to new, brief brightness. He somehow knew that this power was within him, but he could not know for sure when it would come and when it might go. First, however, he would have to touch. Coming in from walks on winter days, he had gone straight to the fire, huddled himself closer and closer to the flames. His mother or his sister had always checked him. Why?'

The question was not directed at Laura. It was as if he were still staring into the fire.

'The coal was the deeper red, so he thought he would begin by touching the flame. Its red was sometimes gold, even a paler yellow. Occasionally – too fleetingly – a magic green. Its flicker and curve drew him forward. He would touch the top of the flame, then slowly move his hand down and pick out the coal. For a moment he felt nothing, then it pierced. A cry, a shout, the rack of drying clothes over-turned, his mother's scolding voice, the agony and delight of the cold water. Later, his father's slow, stern, kind voice. The lesson that could only be learnt through the pain of action and reaction.'

A long silence. She was about to speak when she heard what seemed to be a different voice.

'*Life is a pure flame and we live by an invisible sun within us.*'

Then silence again.

'What was that last thing you said?'

He was blinking now, looking at her.

'That my father said that pain is there for a reason, that it's our body's way of reacting to bad things, so we don't repeat the action that causes them.'

'No, you said something else after that.'

He looked at her, bewildered. 'I don't think I did. I'm sure I didn't.'

'Something about the sun.'

He shook his head. She didn't want to accuse him of lying, but she searched his eyes.

'Well, if I did, I don't remember now. That still sometimes happens. I have a thought and a moment later I forget what it was.'

Perhaps this was so. The inflection of the voice had certainly been different. She would let it go for now. 'That's only to be expected. We'll come back to that problem later. Let's just talk a bit about your memory of the incident with the fire. It's encouraging, isn't it? The first recapturing of your own past. How do you feel about that?'

He took time to weigh his answer. 'I don't feel anything about it. It happened in isolation. The memory came back yesterday afternoon. I've repeated it to you now, so I guess it's here to stay.'

'But what does it mean to you?'

Again he was sluggish. 'Nothing really.'

'I'd be so excited if I were in your position. I mean you've found out something about your family. Your mother and father, brother and sister. As soon as you add some names and places to the faces, we'll know who you are and you'll be able to go home.'

'I won't be able to go to that home. It belonged to my childhood.'

'But you'll go to your family – think how worried about you they must be.'

With deep conviction he said, 'I know in my heart that none of those people are still alive.'

'What makes you so sure of that?'

'I know it in my heart.'

Laura decided to pursue another tack. She asked him if anything now seemed to him odd about the language in which he had described his memory.

He thought about this for a long time, then said No.

'Nothing?'

'Nothing at all.'

This was the moment to challenge him. 'You know that's not true, William.'

He didn't answer.

'Come on, do you seriously think that all the people I see talk about their past in the way you did?'

'I've no idea what they do. I still don't know what you're getting at.'

He wasn't going to budge on this and she wasn't going to give him the answer. Return to it in the next session.

'What about Sally or Sarah – anything else about her?'

'No.'

'And the seven-inch conversation?'

'Either he made it up to annoy me or it was a jumble of words that simply meant I had a fever.'

By saying nothing she made him say something more – 'A conversation doesn't have a length, does it?'

'Of course it does. The length of our conversations is an hour.'

'Fifty minutes,' he said. 'And they're almost up.'

Towards the end of each session she always turned the

31

conversation to the therapy itself. It was the standard way of working towards an acknowledgement of the transference.

'Do you mean to suggest that I'm short-changing you by giving you fifty minutes, not a full hour?'

'Not at all. You've got to have five minutes to write up your notes, or whatever you do, and to get ready for the next one.'

'You make it sound as if I just treat you as if you were on a production line.'

'You're doing your job.'

'Our meetings don't have to be thought of in that way, William. Your memories are precious.' This was to reassure him that she was not the detached clinician. It was also true to what she was feeling. There was something about this man and his words.

She feared that her own choice of word was a slip, that he would misunderstand what she meant by 'precious'. But he had relaxed again and did not pick up on it. She asked him if there was anything else he wanted to talk about before they finished for the morning.

'That thing you said about the difference between child-hood memories and later ones,' he inquired, 'were you saying that the adult ones, when they come, will be like short stories, whereas those of childhood – like yesterday's – are more like brief, image-laden lyric poems?'

Ever since his first utterances, with their oddly precise phrasing, she had been wondering if he was a writer or fancied himself as one. This seemed to clinch it. An idea occurred to her.

She congratulated him on his way of putting it. Then she

went on to explain that in the early days of recovery the problem was usually one of retention. A memory would return, sharp as a sensual impression. By rights it should have been as unforgettable as 'the smell of new-mown grass or baking bread' (did he half-raise his eyebrows, as if the writer in him were thinking 'cliché'?). Like all memories, it would fade as quickly as a smell, but, unlike the smell and the memory of the unimpaired mind, sometimes it could not be recalled subsequently through conscious imaginative effort. The jarred brain was not yet ready for the work of processing, storing and recovering at will.

Laura explained that this was one of the most puzzling recurrent experiences in treating amnesiacs: they would describe some incident from their past with as much detail as if they had not merely an unimpaired memory but an exceptionally acute one, yet asked a few minutes later to repeat what they had just said, they would have no idea what it was they had been talking about. This must have been what happened with the sentence about the sun that he had uttered and then instantly forgotten.

'Some people find that the best way of dealing with this difficulty is to write down everything they remember. Would that appeal to you, William? Keep a pad of paper beside you, and as you remember something, write it down – but you need to develop the knack of catching it in the midst. Once you get off the train of recollection, it'll quickly pull ahead of you and you may not be able to get back on.'

She was convinced that his amnesia no longer had much to do with the head-wound, but it was crucial that he should not know she thought this. Nor that she had other reasons for wanting him to write.

It was agreed that he would write down all his memories and leave his writings for her at the desk in reception, so that she could look them over prior to each session. She had found the supporting therapy that she had promised the team she would come up with in order to speed the process.

4

At nine o'clock on Wednesday morning she took the pages from her pigeonhole and went to her office.

Some sheets of ruled A4. The writing was in fountain pen, neat to begin with, but as she flicked through the pages it looked increasingly scrawled, as if the hand had moved more and more quickly. Had it been written in biro, she thought, it would have been illegible.

On the first line of the first page he had written three words.

Distant objects please.

The rest of the page was blank. She turned to the second. The remaining four pages were full.

This is what she read.

«« »»

'I hope the suggestion appeals to you,' she said. The suggestion did appeal. The very image of a man writing, of myself with pen in hand, became a memory of peculiar force. It felt like a kind of homecoming.

After she told me that our time was up, I went straight to the hospital shop and bought a solid tablet of ruled paper. Two hundred sheets. On the cover of it, there was a picture of a bearded writer. Authors' names and book titles are still a blank area, so his name meant nothing to me, but I hailed him nevertheless as my brother.

My fingers were itching to hold a pen. I wanted one which would feel firm in my hand, but which would have a fine nib. I imagined ink flowing smoothly, being formed into spidery words. To my frustration, I was told that the hospital shop sold only ballpoints. I did not want to preserve my precious fragments of memory with a ballpoint. I was impatient to begin, but could only do so if the conditions were right. Someone had told me at the weekend that the shop sometimes undertook special orders for patients, so I asked the woman if they could obtain a fountain pen and some ink for me. Long experience must have taught her the need for patience in dealing with the curious requests of patients. She said she would try to find out.

She seemed to be away for hours. My sense of duration is still uncertain. At the instant of her return, I detected a half-smile. Condescension or pity, or triumph – the special pleasure known to those who are about to bestow a gift? 'I'm afraid we can't supply a fountain pen,' she began, but the smile assured me that this was not the whole story. 'But I've spoken to OT, and they say they have a supply of good pens and ink for calligraphy classes. They think they'll be able to help you.'

Thanking her I fear too briskly, I hurried out and made for the nearest hospital map. I worked my way down a narrow passage between two shabby portacabins into that marked 'Occupational Therapy'. The person I found there was not the one who had spoken to the woman in the shop. From the report of the conversation, I had imagined the owner of the voice on the phone to be motherly and easy-going, perhaps a teacher of tapestry or raffia-work. This young woman was harassed: her look and her tone seemed to say, Just because we don't have surgical training and hi-tech equipment in Occupational Therapy, that doesn't make us any less pressured. She would have to consult a supervisor, check on the requisitioning procedures. The ink would come under consumables, the pen under equipment. Equipment was not allowed to be removed from the unit, you know. These pens were not for writing home. Biros were available in the hospital shop. If I wanted to improve my handwriting I could sign up for a class, provided my consultant had given me a chit saying I was at an appropriate stage of my treatment to enter OT.

As patiently as I could, I told her of my amnesia and of Mrs Foster's advice. I told her that of course I *could* use a 'biro', but that I would feel so much more able to undertake this work of writing if I had a pen which I liked, which felt as if it had a history. 'I'm sorry to be so much trouble, Miss Pierce,' I said (I had learnt that the best way to get anything in this place was to read the lapel badge, make eye contact, look desperate and use the name), 'but it's a sort of psychological thing – the problem with these memories is that I don't seem to possess them for more than a moment, they seem flimsy and disposable, and that's how those pens in the shop seem too. I want a fountain pen because it can be replenished, because it has its own history.'

I was three-quarters expecting her to tell me to stop wasting her time with such nonsense, but on the contrary she melted and said, 'I quite understand – I love using a proper pen to write to old friends. I'll see what I can do for you. Come back this afternoon.'

Three hours later I was furnished with a heavy fountain

pen and a large box of cartridges. All that was required was a verbal assurance that the pen would be returned when I was discharged, together with my signature at the foot of a triplicate form on which Miss Pierce (who had obviously spoken to someone who had read my file, perhaps Laura herself) had typed 'Unknown, William' under 'Name of Patient'. Under 'Purpose of Requisition' she had put 'Personal Therapeutic Programme: Writing'.

As if writing could be anything but therapeutic.

After I had filled the pen and opened the writing pad, I sat for a long time. At last three words came to me. I slowly formed them. But nothing followed from them.

By then it was time for the evening meal and I was not in the mood to try again afterwards. I'll get started properly in the morning, when I'm fresh, I thought.

So this is my morning's work. I have made myself write, but I have only written about making myself write. Just the three words which haunt me, the phrase hammering until my head aches: *distant objects please*. Why?

Laura will not be pleased, but I'll leave her the pages anyway.

«« »»

She was pleased that he had written her name as Laura.

On the final page, his handwriting had deteriorated so far that she wondered for a moment if it was still his own.

«« »»

No young man believes he shall ever die. It was a saying of my brother's, and a fine one. There is a feeling of eternity in youth, which makes us amends for every thing. To be young is to be as one of the immortal gods. One half of time indeed is flown – the other half remains in store for us with all its countless treasure; for there is no line drawn, and we see no limit to our hopes and wishes. We make the coming age our own.

The vast, the unbounded prospect lies before us.

Death, old age, are words without a meaning, that pass by us like the idle air which we regard not. Others may have undergone, or may still be liable to them – we bear a charmed life which laughs to scorn all such sickly fancies. As in setting out on a delightful journey, we strain our eager gaze forward and see no end to the landscape, new objects presenting themselves as we advance; so, in the commencement of life, we set no bounds to our inclinations, nor to the unrestricted opportunities of gratifying them. We have as yet found no obstacle, no disposition to flag; and it seems that we can go on for ever.

5

'Are you disappointed in me?' he asked, breaking the obligatory opening silence.

She looked at him without speaking.

'I know your plan was that I should wait for some memory to come to me, then write it down, but I thought that if I got into the habit of writing, that might itself bring the memories back.'

'So why do you think I might be disappointed?'

'Because nothing did come back, apart from those three meaningless words.'

This puzzled her. 'What about the saying of your brother's? That was something else from your past, your family. Didn't it make the exercise worthwhile for you?'

It was his turn to look puzzled.

'What saying of my brother's?'

She handed him the final page.

He read it slowly, then looked at her and said, 'I didn't write that.'

She was convinced that he thought he was telling the truth.

Assuring him that she trusted him, she made him examine the handwriting.

He thought for a long time before saying, 'The hand is mine but the words are not.'

She tried to make a connection: 'Have you thought any

more about my question about your choice of words when you described your memory of burning your hand as a child?'

It did not work. He had apparently blanked out the fact that he had spoken of his childhood self as a 'he' and not an 'I'. If the memory was of his childhood self.

She tried to stimulate his memory by starting various lines of conversation from details in his writing. But each time she hit a dead end. She felt a vacancy within him. No progress with free association either.

She probed the question of his sense of duration and ability to estimate time, which in his writing he had said were still shaky. When she tested him on his daily routine and asked him to guess how much of their hour had passed, he replied accurately enough.

She asked about his drinking habits. He looked surprised. She pressed him. He said that he never drank at all, though he had a guilty recollection of occasional breaches of this rule at times of extreme stress. She nodded, explaining that she was only asking because she had to check every possibility, including that of Korsakoff's syndrome, a particular kind of amnesia caused by alcoholism.

She then asked if he had any recollection of having been under particular strain in the period immediately prior to his 'adventure'. He said that he was not aware that he had been – he still had no memories save the distant ones.

'But even if I was, why would it be relevant?'

The hostility was what she expected. It only provided further confirmation of her diagnosis. She did not answer his question directly, telling him instead to keep trying with the writing.

The Cure for Love

There was nearly always a session some time early in a new patient's treatment which achieved absolutely nothing. It was good to get it out of the way so soon. She would try something different on Friday.

6

He began by telling her that he had not remembered anything new. Nor had he felt like writing again.

She made a suggestion. Was she right in supposing that he had been looking into the gas fire in the day room when the memory of the burning had come back to him?

He accepted that this was so.

She proposed that they should try a thought experiment. She persuaded him to move from the chair to the couch.

It would not be hypnosis as such. All she was going to do was recreate in him the state of reverie that had chanced to be so productive the previous Sunday afternoon.

He was willing to go along with her.

'Make yourself as comfortable as you can on the couch. Let your head sink back, your arms and hands lie loosely. Find yourself a spot on the ceiling or high on the wall. Look at it in the way you sometimes look into a fire ... Keep listening carefully to my voice as you focus on the spot. Concentrate on what the spot looks like. You don't need to do anything or not do anything. Just let things happen ... Keep listening to my voice as it goes on. Now the spot's changing. It's radiating, becoming a coal. Just enjoy that, keep staring at it ... You're staring into the fire. You're feeling relaxed now, the relaxation is going down your body in waves, down from the head, coming over you, working its way down, down your neck, your back, the

backs of your legs are so relaxed now, down to your feet
... As you gaze into the fire, the waves are rolling through
you, drowsy and relaxed, relaxed and drowsy.'

She was almost asleep herself. 'Concentrate, Foster,' she
said under her slow breath.

'You're staring into the fire, like you used to do when
you were young ... When you used to stare into the fire,
you would remember. You like remembering. Remember
some other times when you used to stare and remember.'

She let the silence fill the room.

He spoke in the voice with which he had spoken of the
falling clothes and the fire.

'The boy stood in the cathedral. He gazed up at the
monument to Mary Queen of Scots. As he tried to select
and order all that he had learnt of her in school, the events
of the history book kept fading from the eye of his mind.
What passed in review before him instead were fragmentary
images of his own life.'

'Beautiful,' Laura thought, struggling to contain herself.

Then he voiced a list of images.

The auburn hair of an older sister.

The cry of a baby sister. The smell of salt and the
sensation of queasiness on a long Atlantic crossing. A
silence in the home in the first days after the crossing; his
parents' strained faces, Peggy crying, the baby no longer
there.

Walking with his father through the deep New England
snow. The taste of barberries picked on the hillside where
they had lain through the winter under the snow. A carpet
of bluebells in a wood. The dazzling, almost invisible
shimmer of a humming-bird's wing. Then the brightness of

the autumnal light and the deep golden-red of the maple leaves.

A white clapperboard church, with its thin, high spire.

Rows of declensions and conjugations in a Latin grammar book. The play of expression on his father's face as he sat reading.

A farmer who befriended him, walked with him in the fields, showed him how to milk a cow.

Lying face down on the ground so that the grass seemed like tall trees.

The sadness in the eyes of an Indian woman selling jewellery.

His earliest consciousness of fear: a winter's evening when he had gone upstairs alone and by a trick of light his own giant shadow had fallen across a curtain and seemed to him an other, a dark intruder, a tall stranger.

Holding a makeshift fishing rod by a river in Maine on the earliest holiday he could remember.

Living cargo on the passage back to the old world: caged mocking birds, the smell of six foxes in cramped quarters, a metal box with breathing holes and the words 'Danger – Rattlesnake'.

Laura was enchanted by his words. He seemed to inhabit language more comfortably than he fitted in his body.

To begin with, the remembered boy had been a 'he', but at some point – thinking back, she could not recollect exactly when it had happened – he had switched to the first person. There was no doubt that the memories were then his own. He clearly recalled holidays on the Kent coast. Presumably these were during the years after his family returned to England.

The memories were coming back like pulses. Not a constant flow, but a series of intense charges interspersed with pauses.

He remembered the excitement of the night before they left home, the fear that his cricket bat would be left behind. Then the journey itself, at first another excitement, then seemingly interminable. Games of I-spy and eager glances at the roadsigns counting down the number of miles to their destination. The different customs of his grandmother's home: the particular scent of China tea in the front room and an utterly distinctive but now elusive smell in the dining room. Silver tongs for handling sugar cubes at teatime. Gulls screeching overhead as he went to sleep in his narrow bed in the little room at the top of the house – his brother had left home for art school in London, and Peggy was of an age to demand a room to herself. She was ensconced amidst the clutter of the back room which their aunt – who lived with Granny, but was away walking in the Alps – called her 'den'. Oddly, the most vivid memory was not of the beach but of the public gardens at the top of the cliffs.

As the hour came to an end, he was remembering that English had been one of his two favourite subjects at school and that he had always loved the exercise early in the autumn term when the class were told to write about their summer holidays. 'The teacher would tell us that we shouldn't just give a descriptive account, we should try to write about our *feelings*.'

7

She had brought him back gently, telling him that when he awoke he would remember everything he had said. Her elation at what she had achieved was tempered by unease. Had he not said that he did not want others knowing who he was before he knew himself? She had to remind herself that she was doing her job, doing him the best favour in the world, giving him back his identity. Yet when she phoned Amanda that Sunday night she said nothing about William. Amanda never inquired about the patients; she knew that her sister would talk when it was necessary for her to do so.

After waking him from his reverie – telling herself not to think of it as a full-scale hypnotic trance – she had suggested that he should continue with his writing, try to fix on paper the most important of the things he had said whilst gazing into the imaginary fire.

She came in early on Monday morning. Before going to the eight-thirty meeting, she wanted to read what he had produced over the weekend. It was always disorienting to go directly from discussion with colleagues into the first appointment of the week. She recognized that patients needed a regular timetable, but hated the fact that on Mondays she had so little time to compose herself for her nine-thirty.

This time there were about a dozen closely written pages.

She felt exultant. Whether or not what she had done on Friday was a hypnosis, it had made the breakthrough. The door was open.

She settled down and read slowly.

«« »»

When I was a boy, my father used to take me to the Victoria Gardens at the little seaside town where we went to stay with my grandmother. We would play cricket there for hours, taking it in turns to bat and to bowl. Occasionally another boy would join us, probably to my father's relief – a little less ball-retrieving for his own legs, no longer young. But I always preferred it when it was just the two of us.

I think that this memory is my own, but I do not feel secure in the identity of the boy. The child feels like a 'he' and not an 'I'. But as I write the memory back to life or into being, I cannot afford to trust this feeling and make him a third-person rather than a first. I must make myself believe that he is me. Otherwise I will have nothing. I must ask Laura whether I spoke of an 'I' or a 'he' when I lay on her couch.

Then I hear the voice again, the voice which spoke of the feeling of immortality in youth.

Now the place is deserted, its borders and its beds overturned. Is there, then, nothing that can bring back that place, that time, my father? Perhaps: for when I unlock my memory, this scene of boyhood pleasures still lives unfaded. A new sense comes upon me, as in a dream; a richer perfume, brighter colours start out; my eyes dazzle; my heart heaves with its new load of bliss, and I am a child again. I see the beds of larkspur with purple eyes; tall hollyhocks, red and yellow; the broad sunflowers, caked in gold, with bees buzzing round them; wildernesses of pinks, and hot-glowing peonies; the box-tree borders; the gravel walks; the painted bandstand – I think I see them now with sparkling looks. Or have they vanished while I have been writing this description of them? No matter, they will return again when I least think of them. All that I have observed since, of flowers and plants, and grass plots, and of suburban delights, seems to me borrowed from that pleasure garden of my youth, to be slips and scions stolen from that bed of memory.

In this manner the dear memories of our childhood burnish out in the eye of after-years. If I have pleasure in a municipal flower garden, I have it in a vegetable garden too, and for the same reason. If I see a row of cabbage plants or of peas or beans coming up, I immediately think of those I used so carefully to water of an evening in Shropshire, when my day's tasks were done, and of the pain with which I saw them droop and hang down their leaves in the morning sun.

Again, I never see a child's kite in the air, but it seems to pull at my heart. I feel the twinge at my elbow, the flutter and palpitation, with which I used to let go the string of my own, as it rose in the air and towered among the clouds.

I think that this memory, too, is my own. But now I do not feel secure in the identity of the voice. When Laura showed me the previous words I'd written in that voice, I denied that they were mine. But I *did* write them. When the voice comes to me, what it says is real and is mine. Yet

49

when I make a conscious effort to reconstruct my past, I want to write of 'him'. I struggle to believe that I am remembering myself. What does this mean, Laura?

«« »»

Laura scribbled some notes. It was as if she were trying to answer his question by conducting a written conversation with him.

'Confusion between different self-images. Security in a distant voice, uncertainty about closer one. Compare shift from "he" to "I" in course of hypnosis. Reasons? Tendency of amnesiacs to recover distant past before recent. Possibility of multiple personality?'

She struck out the last comment. The profession was sceptical of Jekyll and Hyde stories. So it had been stressed in her training.

She half-wanted to go with the possibility of dual personality for the exact reason that her teachers would have discouraged her from doing so. She crossed out 'hypnosis' and wrote 'reverie' instead. The word was growing on her.

Then she carried on reading.

«« »»

Home was a market town in Shropshire, a house with low ceilings, father always stooping. Dark panelling, the snug parlour. Father had no money to spare, but Mother and Margaret – Peggy, everyone called her – made it a warm, bustling place. The silence of death which had afflicted the house in New England years earlier was by then forgotten or at least well buried. There was a windowseat on which I read for hours at a time. From it I could see my father's vegetable garden and the rolling hills beyond.

In the summertime I would play in the garden or walk on the hills. I loved to fly my kite.

Once I looked closely at a daisy and realized that it was a fragile thing, easily destroyed by my foot.

Often I watched the thistledown rise and wondered where it would travel. I imagined that one day I would travel the world myself.

Sometimes on winter Sundays I would go up to my parents' room and peep out of the little window that overlooked the chapel next door. The twinkling light and murmuring voices made me feel warm.

Religion and politics. That's what Father always talked about.

I did not really understand politics, but I knew from what Father told me that there were good men and bad men, that the good men fought for freedom and justice and energetic life, while the bad men were old and grey and wielded hammers with which they dealt blows against – father's favourite phrase, one which always had him slamming his hand down on the table, clenching his fist in a gesture of purpose, or flushing with pride – 'our great tradition of radical dissent'. The five years abroad had been forced upon us by something to do with Father's politics.

Now I remember the moment at which I began to have my own thoughts about public affairs. Thirteen years old, I went away from home alone for the first time. Father had thought that this would be character-forming, and arranged for me to stay with an old friend from what he called his 'hot youth'. Dr Shepherd was a towering man with a great hooked beak of a nose. He ministered to a dwindling congregation in Gateacre, a run-down area of Liverpool near a huge car factory. From his pulpit he fulminated against the bosses and the government. As a political partisan, no one could stand against him.

Dr Shepherd's greatest hero was John Bunyan. A preacher for the people.

With his brandished club, like the Giant Despair in 'The Pilgrim's Progress', he knocked out his opponents' brains. Not only no individual, but no corrupt system, neither government nor capitalist enterprise, could hold out against his powerful and repeated attacks; but with the same weapon, swung round like a flail, with which he levelled his antagonists, he laid his friends low and put his own party out of action. If his blows had been straight forward and steadily directed to the same object, no unpopular boss could have lived before him; instead of which he laid about right and left, impartially and remorselessly, made a clear stage, had all the ring to himself, and then ran out of it, just when he should have stood his ground.

The shop stewards refused to work with him.

Dr Shepherd's lack of measure made me admire my own father's political instincts. When I returned home and father asked me what I thought of old Shepherd, I replied that he seemed a very honest man but one totally lacking in principle. Father was puzzled by this, but nodded warmly when I explained the paradox by saying that Dr Shepherd 'appeared to be in downright earnest in all he said, in the part he took at any one time, but in taking that part he was

led entirely by headstrong obstinacy, pique or personal
motive of some sort, and not by a steadfast regard for truth
or habitual anxiety for justice.' The judgement may well
have pleased him because its distinctive turns of phrases –
'downright earnest', 'steadfast regard', 'habitual anxiety' –
were his own.

My happiest time in Liverpool was an afternoon spent
walking on the sands at New Brighton with Dr Shepherd's
daughter, Sally. At one point we cut across some rocks
covered with smooth, bright green seaweed, and Sally
slipped and I steadied her, then held her hand for a little
longer than was strictly necessary. As I looked out towards
the mouth of the river, the sky was beautiful, with mackerel
clouds stretched across it. Beyond was the sea, which always
made me think of time and eternity, constancy and hope.
But when I stood by the fort – built in the time of Napoleon,
Sally tentatively informed me – and turned my gaze back
over the Mersey to the docks, I was cast into deep gloom.
The sun went in, the wind suddenly picked up and everything was grey. Ships, cranes, drudgery.

The next day Dr Shepherd took me to a party in a flat
belonging to a fellow clergyman who lived in the centre of
Liverpool. As he drove through the city at a fearsome speed,
veering sharply to left and right in the avoidance of pot-
holes, I was cast down still further by the sight of decaying
buildings, boarded-up windows, pinched faces on the street.
The women were pale, always frowning. Some of the girls
pushing babies seemed no older than myself. The flat was
in a crumbling Regency mansion, incongruously located
opposite a tower block (new, but also crumbling) in an area

known by its postal code, 'Liverpool 8'. Years later I think I caught a glimpse of the building's cream stonework in some television news footage of rioting youths.

Two things stood out at the party: the main room's huge painted wooden fireplace with great pillars down either side, like something from a stage set, and an overheard fragment of conversation. One of the other guests, darker-skinned than the rest, was introducing himself as the owner of a neighbouring flat in the building. He said, 'You know these mansions were built by slave owners – well, I was brought up in the area and when I was a young scally I used to walk past and vow that one day I'd live here to take something back for my people.'

I thought: so here is a descendant of a slave. Perhaps his ancestors escaped as the ship waited in dock for the tide to turn. But then I checked myself. To my boy's imagination, slavery meant romantic images of sailing ships, stowaways and sugar plantations. So what about the docks I'd looked towards the previous day and the strained faces of the people seen from the car? There were no more slave-masters cracking whips, but the world was still divided into those who had and those who didn't. Dock labourers with greased and blackened hands, girls who got pregnant because they saw no other future. Still enslaved.

And so, after this visit, I began to have the confidence to interject questions and tentative opinions when Father spoke over dinner about politics and the great events of the day. I think that Father came to respect his son's quiet but firm voice; the two of us drew closer together. To us, the bond of politics was all male; it pulled me away from my mother and my sister.

One evening over family dinner Mother asked me what I had done in school that day. I said: 'I read the best thing I've ever read.' My father looked surprised – the reply had come with such speed, such uncompromising certainty. He was even more surprised when I continued, 'I'll recite some of it to you. Listen.' Before Peggy or either of my parents had time to ask whether I'd been told to learn a passage or had simply taken it upon myself to do so because I liked it so much, I was off.

'From this time forward the event became more certain every round; and about the twelfth it seemed as if it must have been over. Hickman generally stood with his back to me; but in the scuffle, he had changed positions, and Neate just then made a tremendous lunge at him, and hit him full in the face. It was doubtful whether he would fall backwards or forwards; he hung suspended for a second or two, and then fell back, throwing his hands in the air, and with his face lifted up to the sky. I never saw anything more terrific than his aspect just before he fell. All traces of life, of natural expression, were gone from him. His face was like a human skull, a death's head, spouting blood. The eyes were filled with blood, the nose streamed with blood, the mouth gaped blood. He was not like an actual man, but like a preternatural, spectral appearance, or like one of the figures in Dante's *Inferno*. Yet he fought on after this for several rounds, still striking the first desperate blow, and Neate standing on the defensive and using the same cautious guard to the last, as if he had still all his work to do; and it was not until the Gas-man was so stunned in the seventeenth or eighteenth round, that his senses forsook him, and he could not come to time, that the battle was declared over. Ye who despise the Fancy, do something to show as much pluck, or as much self-possession as this, before you assume a superiority which you have never given a single proof of by any one action in the whole course of your lives!'

The violence was not to the family's taste. My father deplored the shedding of the blood of any man or beast. Yet somehow I had electrified them with the vigour of the description. Peggy asked what the Fancy was, and I replied, in a schoolboy's knowing way, that it was an old word for prizefighting. Not that I had known this before the morning's English lesson.

Though the repeated images of blood had made my mother feel sick, she could not forbear to ask how long it had taken me to learn the extract. I replied that I hadn't learnt the passage at all, that I'd only read it that day in class, and looked over it again a couple of times while doing my homework. 'It's always like that with things I read and really like – if they matter to me enough, they go into my head and stay there.'

I do not think that this evening has returned to me because it was the first occasion on which I heard the phrase 'photographic memory' used for this capacity which I once had (I don't believe that it will ever come back to me – when I read something now, I find it hard to take it in as far as the end of the page; the idea of it sticking in my mind so that I could spout it out again later is impossible to comprehend). No, what was important was my sympathy for the writer of the words. The passage I recalled was the moment that stood out from my first acquaintance with what was to become the strongest of the voices. That I cannot now remember the name of the author is as frustrating as the uncertainty I still feel about my own name.

I think that I would have been about fifteen years old. Among my set books at school was an anthology of essays which my teacher had put together himself. Somehow the texts were more immediate for being typewritten, cyclostyled and stapled, not printed and bound. I liked the clarity of an essay about shooting an elephant, but best of all I liked the one about the prizefight. And this moment, the moment when Mr Thomas Hickman, known in the ring as the Gas-man, stood like something preternatural and you didn't know which way he was going to fall, was the most memorable of all. It was one of the first times I had seen what good writing could do, how it could make a moment – an action, a feeling – that is long past, or that never happened, seem like something we have witnessed, something we have felt.

As soon as I had swallowed the essay into the digestive system of my imagination, my instincts told me that I had been at the fight. I had not read about the Gas-man's fall, I had seen it. I had felt the ground shudder and participated in the crowd's collective intake of breath. And I had come under the intoxicating influence of a certain style: from that time on, my own thinking and writing would often be flavoured with pugilistic metaphor.

In a way it was strange that I was so impressed by this particular piece of writing, for I hated boxing, was so scared the only time I was made to try it that I took revenge on the teacher by writing a pompous article in the school magazine denouncing compulsory sports. Which was itself a strange thing to do, because there were other games that I loved, because to time a wristy backhand on the squash court is one of the most satisfying experiences I know, because the June day I spent with my father at Lord's watching Sir Garfield Sobers score a magnificent century was possibly the day of the most unalloyed bliss in my life. One square drive in particular: no time seemed to separate the click of bat against ball from the smack of ball against boundary board. My father and I turned our heads to each other; we did not have to speak to express the purity of our shared delight; in the evening, walking with the crowd back to the tube, he said that he had not seen such timing since Hammond.

I suspect that it was to make up for my impulsive attack on the sporting life that years later I wrote an article in praise of squash for some magazine.

It may be said that there are things of more importance than striking a ball against a wall – there are things indeed which make more noise and do as little good, such as making war and peace, making speeches and answering them, making sentences and blotting them, making money and throwing it away. But no one who has ever played the game of squash despises it. It is the finest exercise for the body, and the best relaxation for the mind. He who takes to playing at squash is twice young. He feels neither the past nor the future in the instant. Debts, taxes, nothing can touch him further. He has no other wish, no other thought, from the moment the game begins, than that of striking the ball, of placing it, of making it.

The editor particularly liked the touch about making money and throwing it away; he said that it sounded the authentic note of the *Zeitgeist*, which was almost enough to make me withdraw the article. But I needed the money.

I know that the white box of the squash court was sometimes my only place of refuge in difficult times, but can I now be sure that I did write that article? Or did I read it and make it my own, thanks to the curse of my photographic memory? Have I remembered the words or have I created them at this moment? And whose words are they?

If someone picks up this pad on which I have been writing, takes in the words and takes the thought to heart, do the words not then belong to them and no longer to me? It is when I start having thoughts like these that I imagine Laura's diagnosis is wrong: I do not have post-traumatic amnesia, I am going mad.

Sometimes, at times such as this, I do not think I belong here. For sometimes I know I am elsewhere. But then it is not a question of place, for it has always been important to me that I should inhabit a place. When I move into a room, whether it is a hotel for one night or a lodging in which I will live for as long as it takes me to need to move on, the first thing I do is arrange it. I do not like to live out of my trunk, so I unpack my books, my clothes. I find a place for my few engravings and postcards: a landscape, reproductions of three old masters, figures of my heroes. I prefer rooms that have a mantelpiece, but sometimes I have to prop the curling images on desk or dressing table. Where are those pictures now?

And on the first day in each new place, I walk. Like an animal marking the bounds of its territory, I orient myself. If it is a city or town, I find the nearest park or public garden. The sight and the memory of little spots of green, even of odd trees on the street, are my landmarks. Through them, I know that I belong in a place, that I am not alone, that there is another world besides my inner one.

But still I feel that I am not where I am. Perhaps, then, it is a matter of time not place. I am not elsewhere but elsewhen. When I am in the theatre, the world on stage is more real to me than that in the auditorium. Is that so unusual? I feel then that I live in a time of heroes. Princes, Moors and Thanes. *I have had more pleasure in reading the adventures of a novel (and perhaps changing situations with the hero) than I ever had in my own.*

I never stop hearing the voices. Their voices, the voices of the past, of heroes, of plays and novels. I can't stop quoting because the voices are inside me. They *are* me. My very being is woven by them, by what I have read. Often I do not know when I am quoting and when I am speaking in my own voice, but that is a distinction which has no meaning, for my voice is theirs.

Unable to quieten them, I cannot sleep. So I write.

One of the voices is the most insistent of all. It has been speaking within me ever since it dawned on me as I read the essay about the fight, that the people who inhabited my solitary imaginative life had come to me from places without, that they were not all – as, when a younger child, I had imagined them to be – invented by me. And when that one voice speaks above the babble of the many voices, I feel sane and safe, for it lets me know that I am not alone, that this friend is always within me. And he holds together the other voices, brings them to order, sometimes interprets them for me.

Sometimes he seems to be my father, but more often he sounds the words of a more distant past. And his words, like mine, are frequently not his own but those of the voices he must have heard. He, too, often thinks of his father. He has let me piece together his life and his family and I have come to fancy that my life may be but a distorted echo of his. But what I do not know is this: whether he has achieved immortality by living in me or whether he has been dissolved for ever and the truth is only that fragments of his being have been reincarnated or reconstituted in me.

And is it his being or his words? And does he – do I – have any kind of being behind or beyond the words? Nor do I know whether his survival, if that is what it is, guarantees mine or prevents it.

'Keep it simple,' I say to myself. 'The first thing you can do to sort this out is find out his name. Put a name to the witness of the prizefight and you will have made a beginning.' But nobody here in the hospital can help me, and the library does not seem to have any books from the past.

8

Laura put down the final page. She was usually at her best early in the morning, but now she felt exhausted.

She looked at her watch. Twenty to nine – damn it. It was a matter of pride that she should never be late for the team meeting. Dishevelled intrusion without apology was Bill Braddock's trademark.

She apologized to Andrews, but found it impossible to concentrate on the cases that were being discussed. When asked about progress with 'William', she informed her colleagues that he had made an excellent start and that she had got him writing about his past as well as talking about it in the sessions. She kept the puzzling features to herself – the business about 'I' and 'he'; the 'other voice' with its strangely old-fashioned idiom; the fact that the memories appeared to be coming back in chronological sequence, beginning with childhood, as if he were suffering from organic amnesia and not the psychogenic condition which was generally agreed upon.

She held up the sheaf of papers. 'He's produced some very rich material here.'

Bill Braddock pitched in: 'But not, I suppose, anything so rich as his surname, his address or his social security number?'

She replied crisply, 'I've thought about confabulation, but I'm convinced he's not a malingerer.' Her instincts always told her when someone was lying. His words under hypnosis could not have been faked.

Braddock looked sceptical; Andrews told her to keep up the good work and give a more detailed report the following week.

«« »»

'Did you have time to read all that?'

So direct a question had to be answered. A bad start to the week: he had disrupted her technique of not speaking before he had spoken twice.

'Yes, thank you. You've certainly given us a lot to talk about. How well do you yourself remember what you've written?'

'Most of it. But, as I said, I can't imagine ever having a photographic memory again, if that is what I had.'

'Do you think it is what you had?'

'The term seemed right.'

'Seemed?'

'Don't you find it funny treating an amnesiac who claims to have a photographic memory?'

She did not answer this question. She had developed the knack of knowing when an extra moment's silence would turn the conversation in a more productive direction.

William said: 'Could you tell from the writing when it was that I was hearing a voice, not remembering something for myself?'

Still she did not reply.

He continued, 'I mean, a voice inside me – not a voice coming from the walls or out of the television when it's turned off.' They both knew what he meant. There was a

63

classic schizophrenic in the ward who heard voices of that kind.

'Are you worried about the voices?'

'I think I would be if there were a cacophony of them. Then I'd be like someone with a hearing aid who struggles at parties. But because most of the time it's just the one voice I feel more reassured than anything else.'

'Why do you think that voice makes you feel secure?'

'As I wrote. Because he reminds me of my father.'

'What was your father's job, William?'

'I'm not sure – teacher, preacher?'

'Can you remember his full name – Reverend, Doctor, Mister . . .'

William replied more quickly than usual: 'I'm still getting nowhere with names.'

'Except for Peggy?'

'Except for Peggy.'

'So why do you think you can remember your sister's name and no one else's?'

He did not know why. And why did he never remember any surnames?

'When my memories come back, it's as if they're like dreams. People in dreams never have surnames.' Too glib, thought Laura, though it struck her how much time she spent with patients talking about their loved and hated ones, always using Christian names for all these people she had never met.

She challenged him. 'You're never specific about places either, are you?'

'I've written all I can remember.'

She tried a different tack, playing the role of his ally:

'What do you think I ought to say if a sceptical colleague proposes that you're deliberately withholding things you have remembered, to prevent us from knowing who you really are?'

'Because in reality I'm a serial killer on the run?'

She smiled. A tacit signal thus passed between them: we will not, for the moment, play the game of trying to outsmart each other in this area.

'Hypnotize me again,' he said.

'I wouldn't exactly call it hypnosis,' she corrected.

'But you'd grant that it worked – and I could see that you felt excited about it when I came round.'

'If you want me to hypnotize you again, as you call it, there must be something else you want to tell me. Do you think we know each other well enough by now for you to tell it to me directly, without the rigmarole on the couch?'

'Rigmarole on the couch?' he echoed, with a grin. She wanted to giggle, but let it pass. This was not the moment to address the transference.

'Come on, William. There *are* colleagues who think you're wasting our time here. Why don't you just say what's on your mind?'

'I don't know what's on my mind. I just suggested that you should hypnotize me again so that you could be sure I wasn't making things up.'

'No one has said you're making things up. And people very frequently fantasize when under hypnosis, so that wouldn't prove anything anyway.'

'Oh, forget it, then.'

'Why are you angry with me?'

'Don't start on that one, Laura. I'm not one of your

regulars. I do know all that stuff about transferring the emotion on to the analyst.'

Progress! 'But, William, I thought you were very insistent that I'm not your shrink, that we're not to treat this like psychotherapy, that all we're doing is getting your memory back?'

'Exactly, and the way we're going to do it is through hypnosis.' He stood up from the chair and went to lie down on the couch.

'It's a little unusual for you to be the one to decide what approach we will adopt.'

'You have a reputation for liking unorthodox methods.'

She wondered who he had been talking to. Then she decided that she would simply let him have his way. No matter if he had some defences that meant he could speak of intimate things only when pretending to be under hypnosis. Best to flush out the material, then work to get beyond it. And she had to admit that she liked the rigmarole on the couch.

She repeated Friday's patter, phrase for phrase.

Once his eyelids had dropped, she said, 'It's the day of your first meeting with Sally. Tell me all about it.' She decided on Sally rather than Sarah because that had been the name of the girl in the account of his visit to Liverpool.

This time he spoke from the start of his past self as 'I' instead of 'he'.

'Being at a boys' school, that's the trouble. When I was younger, I was very close to Peggy, but the gap of years between us gradually grew wider and now it's unbridgeable. I'm not exactly in the partying crowd, so I never speak to girls. We're not a musical family and I've got no sense of rhythm. Nothing embarrasses me more than the thought of myself dancing, so I'm dreading tonight. I've never been to the end-of-term disco before. The one occasion on which girls appear in the school. But Elder's persuaded me to go this time. He's been my best friend since we went into the sixth form. God, I envy him – the ease with which he moves between the lads who go to pubs and the bookish boys like me.

'I arrive far too early. "Uncool," comments Elder in the one brief conversation he spares me upon his own fashionably late arrival. For the first two hours I don't know what to do with myself. I strike up conversations with half-friends, but these quickly fizzle out. It seems an age before anyone begins dancing or enough people are in the hall to confer any kind of anonymity. Girls stand around in intimidatingly large groups, raucous, self-confident in their clans, giggly. I keep thinking that they are laughing at me. I fantasize about finding a soul mate, a quiet girl to whom I can quote poetry.

'I'm having a miserable time. I only dare to expose what I describe to Elder as my Terpsichorean ineptitude when the dance floor is so crowded that I can hardly move. I resort to going out and coming back in as if I've only just arrived, but once it reaches eleven o'clock this is no longer possible, since, as a measure against undesirables, nobody is to be allowed in after this time. I know it's the custom that as the evening comes towards its close, slow dances become more frequent. My only hope is to contrive to be in proximity to an isolated girl when one of these begins. But the tactic isn't working.

'I'm just deciding to give up, go home and read a book

when the coloured lights flicker to their dimmer level. The image of the book's open page has been before me, so I don't see the two girls beside me. One of them pairs off immediately, leaving her friend momentarily lost. Before I have time to think about making a fool of myself, I'm asking her if she'd like to dance, she's accepting with manifest relief – Any port in a storm, I guess she's thinking – and I'm holding a girl for the first time in my life.

'How slender she seems, how fragile. I sway with her, holding her by the waist, one hand each side. My out-stretched fingers almost meet around her back. She has placed her hands lightly on my shoulders. I don't dare try to hold her too close. She's eager to talk. Words force a distance between us, stave off more intimate contact.

'Her name is Fenella. Fenella Gifford. Her elder brother is at the school, she tells me. I reply that he's in my Art class. This puts Fenella at her ease. I do not add that I cordially loathe Gifford. First we clashed over politics. The school held a mock election and Gifford orchestrated the press campaign for the Tory, who won easily, while I led that for the Lib-Lab candidate – everyone knew that most of the boys would slavishly follow their parents' votes, so it had been decided that there was no point in splitting the meagre opposition. Then there was an Art lesson in which we had to comment on each other's work. Gifford said that my problem was that I could draw quite accurately but I had no imagination. I instantly vowed to myself that one day I would be a painter praised by the best critics for my strong imagination. Then I'd send a press clipping to Gifford, who would probably have grown up to be a stockbroker.

'When the song ends, I thank Fenella and she gives me a

68

half-smile. I expect her to take the opportunity to escape, but she stays with me. We dance some more, vigorously now, more relaxed because we're not touching each other. In the brighter light, I see her properly. She has very straight, very fine, shoulder-length black hair, parted in the middle. Her face is pale, pixie-like. She's wearing black trousers and a white blouse, the top three buttons undone.

'After a while, she says she has to be excused. I assume that this is the excuse to leave. The thought must show in my face because she says she'll be back in a moment. The wait is agonizingly long. First, I can't see her at all. Then she's in the far corner of the hall with her brother. Voices are being raised, and not just because of the volume of the music. Then another boy from my class, Hunt, is pushing his way across the room.

'Hunt's words: Gifford says that if you put your hand up his sister's shirt, he'll knife you – she's only fourteen. I'd no idea passions could run so high so easily. I'm beginning to enjoy myself. Hunt slides away without waiting for a reply; Fenella is struggling across the crowded dance floor. With perfect timing, she reaches me as the lights turn blue for another slow number, the last of the evening. She's slightly flushed from the row with her brother. This time we dance with our arms fully round each other. My hand is over the thin strap that runs across her back beneath her shirt. I press myself against her. She doesn't flinch, even though she must be aware of my stiffening. I can feel the give of her breasts against my lower chest. I'm a lot taller than her. I smell her hair – apple? – and close my eyes. Harry Nilsson is howling, *Can't live, if living is without you.*

'As the music fades, we disentwine and look at each

other. We incline, as if to kiss, but one or the other or both of us turn aside a split second before the plunge.'

William, stretched on the couch, fell silent.

Laura, who had been completely absorbed in the details of his story, panicked for a moment – she did not want him to end here. She was reliving the nightmare of school dances in her own teenage years. Those damned spots. On an impulse she thought she would try acting out within the hypnosis.

'Thank you for the dance,' she said.

Seamlessly he replied, 'Can I walk you home?'

She second-guessed Fenella's response: 'I'll have to ask my brother.'

William then described another heart-pounding wait. Yes, Fenella told him, he could walk her home, but she had to be in no more than ten minutes after her brother.

Laura did not need to intervene again. She listened and the night became as real to her as if it were her own memory.

'It's all too short a distance to Fenella's house, three-quarters of a mile down the hill. She says that it's cold. I put my arm round her shoulder and walk as slowly as possible. It's a clear, frosty night. Lots of stars, I say. Yes, is her only word. We say nothing more. We reach the end of her drive. The houses here are set back from the road, much larger than those in my part of town.

'She thanks me for a nice evening. I ask if I can kiss her goodnight, cursing myself, sure that Elder would not have asked but just done it. She doesn't answer for a moment, then says that she supposes I can. Neither of us seems to know how to get our head into position, but after one false start our lips meet. Her mouth is hot and at first strangely hollow. I like it when our tongues perform a little dance, but then she breaks away.

'Unable to think of anything to say, I nuzzle her hair and blow on her ear lobe. She seems to like this, so I risk a second kiss. Her hands had stayed still the first time, but now she ruffles my hair as her tongue probes. I take this as a cue to go further and fumblingly undo her coat. I place my hand on her right breast. I am more conscious of the outline of laced cotton beneath the shirt than of the pubescent breast itself. Before I have the opportunity to take my chance with her brother's knife, she's pushing me away.'

Laura knew that time was running short, but she did not want to break in too soon. William was playing both parts in the dialogue. It was perfectly clear which words had been his and which Fenella's, even though his tone did not alter, as it did when he spoke in what Laura described to herself as the *distant voice*.

'I must go in now, or my brother'll kill me.'

'Can I phone you?'

'I suppose so.'

'What's your number?'

'It's in the book.'

'OK then.'

'There's an awkward pause, then as she turns to scurry up the drive she says, "I've never been kissed before – and that." I am touched by the vulnerability in this, and want to hold her. I walk home, with no memory of her taste.

'When I find out what's on at the cinema, I telephone, my palms sweating. The mother answers. "I'll see if she's in." Wouldn't she know her daughter's whereabouts? When she returns: "No, I'm afraid she's not. Can I take a message?" I give my name and number and a message for Fenella to ring me. After I put the receiver down, I convince myself that, to judge from the length of time the mother was away from the phone and the hushed voices I was sure I'd heard, Fenella had been at home but had declined to speak to me – or been commanded not to. Because of her age? Surely not because of my politics?

'There's no return call until Tuesday. My mother beats me to the phone. She calls up as I hover at the top of the stairs; I race down, three steps at a time. Fenella says that she had a very nice evening, but she's afraid she won't be able to go out with me. I put down the phone. "*What* was her name?" asks my mother. "It sounded like Vanilla Goatherd." I tell her that the call was nothing, just someone involved with my community service project. I return to my book. I do not go to any more discos.'

There was silence.

Laura knew that this was her cue to 'wake' him, first telling him that he would remember everything that he had said. She also reckoned she knew that since the story was told in the form of 'I' and not 'he', it was his own story.

William passed through – or did he feign? – a gradual recovery of consciousness and a period of reflection. Then he congratulated Laura, telling her she had been right that there would be islands of memory in a sea of oblivion. He expressed amazement and satisfaction at how every detail of that Saturday evening was clear. At how all the names were there: Elder, Fenella, Gifford, Hunt. But around the island, he claimed, there was still nothing. Nothing of his own surname, of Sarah or Sally.

Time was up and Laura was annoyed, but couldn't show it. She had let him take control of the rhythm of the session. He had contrived to finish his story a mere five minutes before the end, leaving no time for subsequent analysis.

Calmly, she congratulated him on what he had remembered. Testing him, she suggested that Fenella Gifford could be traced through her Health Service records – the name was uncommon enough. This was the kind of lead they had been waiting for: now they could establish his home town, his school and thus the elusive surname. Then she said, 'Or perhaps we'll try another form of hypnosis next time, the sort my colleague Mr Braddock recommended in the first place – it just involves making you drowsy with a chemical instead of with words. But maybe that won't be necessary, if the writing goes well.'

9

Thinking through the case in her bath on Tuesday evening, Laura had concluded, first, that he had feigned the previous day's hypnotic trance and, secondly, that it had been a bad move to play his game, a worse one to act out Fenella Gifford's words, and worst of all to allow his story to enter her imagination.

She had been taught a lot about the counter-transference. The most important thing was to be aware of it. With hindsight it was easy to see that her fleeting desire to be Fenella Gifford was but a transferential effect of the intimacy of the analytic situation. But it was alarming that she had not been fully conscious of this at the time.

She had no intention of tracing Fenella Gifford. She was not even particularly concerned whether or not the story had been true. It did not matter whether 'William' was remembering or confabulating. Her interest was not in his past for its own sake, but in the reasons for his repression of it and the emotional effects of his remembering or storytelling.

It would have been possible to phone round Edinburgh hotels and police stations in search of his movements before the fugue. 'A tall, rather gaunt man in his late thirties or early forties, with dark, slightly curly hair and a pronounced frown, who walked out of a hotel or guest house round about such and such a day, probably not paying his bill,

but leaving behind his luggage, his jacket and his wallet.'
But that was not the point. Only if he recovered his identity
himself, with the aid of the dual therapy of talking and
writing, would the cure be effected. Only if he came to an
admission of why he walked out of his own life would he
be able to walk back into it.

Still, she now thought that he was not sufficiently trau-
matized to merit an in-patient place. It was time to put on
the pressure and move towards a discharge and weekly
therapy on an out-patient basis.

Early on Wednesday morning she read the next body of
writing. It was twice as long as the previous one. About
thirty unnumbered pages. She intended only to skim it for
names and places. But she could not stop herself from
getting interested in the story. She liked the sound of the
'voice' which periodically punctuated his reminiscences. As
he had said himself, it seemed comforting. To her ear it
sounded more authentic, as well as more stylish, than his
own voice. She caught herself becoming another Amanda:
reading a case history for the sake of descriptive detail more
than psychological insight.

This is what she read.

«« »»

School reports noted my relish for words. 'Possible career
in journalism?', one of them queried. But, probably out of
a desire to imitate my admired brother, I threw myself most
wholeheartedly into my Art classes.

*One of my first attempts was a picture of my father. I
drew it with a broad light crossing the face, looking down,
with spectacles on, reading. The sketch promised well and I*

75

set to work to finish it, determined to spare neither time nor pains. My father was willing to sit as long as I pleased, for there is a natural desire in the mind of man to sit for one's picture, to be the object of continued attention, to have one's likeness multiplied – and besides his satisfaction in the picture, he had some pride in the artist, even though he would rather his son should have written a political pamphlet than painted like Cézanne. Those winter days, with the gleams of sunshine coming through the windows, feeling cheered by the notes of the robin in the garden as my afternoon's work drew to a close, were among the happiest of my life. When I gave the effect I intended to any part of the picture for which I had prepared my colours, when I imitated the roughness of the skin by a lucky stroke of the pencil, when I hit the clear pearly tone of a vein, when I gave the ruddy complexion of health, the blood circulating under the broad shadows of one side of the face, I thought my fortune made, or rather it was already more than made in my fancying that I might one day be able to say as Correggio once said, 'I also am a painter.' It was an idle thought, a boy's conceit; but that did not make me less happy at the time. I used regularly to set my work in the chair to look at it through the long evenings; and many a time did I return to take leave of it before I could go to bed at night.

Inevitably, when the time came to leave school, I followed my brother's path to art college in London. One had to begin with a so-called foundation year before proceeding to a degree-level course. Having always lived in small towns, I didn't like the noise and dirt and pace of London. Not that I could have afforded to go out on the town if

I'd wanted to: by the time I'd paid the rent, there was hardly anything left of my student grant. But after a month or so I began to enjoy my independence. I grew my hair. I transformed my wardrobe, courtesy of charity shops and weekend markets. I cultivated an air of languor, occasionally punctuated with bursts of impassioned energy. I fell in love. I made myself an ostentatiously difficult member of the class, always asking the theoretical question where others were content to cultivate their technique.

I did not socialize much with the other students. They all seemed to have more money than I did and they never wanted to talk about great art. The height of their ambitions seemed to be a future in graphic design, which was a way of saying that they wanted to go into the burgeoning, prosperous worlds of advertising or fashion.

The one person I saw with some frequency was Elder, who had come to London to study philosophy at the university. By chance, we had lodgings within walking distance of each other. Two or three evenings a week we would meet and talk over mug after mug of tea (me) or coffee from a cup and saucer (Elder). Sometimes we would arrange to work till ten, then meet for a chat; sometimes we would talk until eleven and then go to a late-night movie; often our conversations would last until four or five, and when I walked home through the city there were occasional moments of blessed silence – even, once, the sound of birdsong.

Always impressionable and competitive, I now spent more and more time reading the great philosophers. I slept little. If I wasn't staying up late talking to Elder, I was sitting over a book, grappling with a line of reasoning which I hadn't been formally trained to follow. Sometimes there was a burning sensation in my head and everything turned to bright blankness. At other times, the sensation was sweet. One night I really thought that I'd grasped an essential idea in Kant and it made me feel as if I knew the meaning of the word Enlightenment.

The philosophy also set me thinking about the politics I'd inherited from my father. The essential question here was whether man was innately selfish or innately benevolent. My own instincts and inheritance made me want to believe the latter, but Elder always argued ferociously for the former, reaching over to his bookshelf and triumphantly reading out great swathes of Hobbes and Mandeville. One damp evening, huddled over my gas fire, I had a vivid memory of my own childhood. I looked into the fire and thought as hard as I could for an hour. The next night I tried out a new argument on Elder. 'If a child burns itself, it will not go too near an open flame again. Why should that be?'

'Self-preservation, old boy, a natural instinct, perfectly consistent with the theory of the innate self-regard of the human mind.'

'But it's not the present self that the child is preserving. What it's doing is *imagining* the future self. It is entering sympathetically into the life of a being that does not actually exist. That's not pure self-interest. Now if the mind has this innate capacity to feel for the imagined future self in this way, then it also has the capacity to feel for imagined other selves. Feeling precedes the formation of the self and the principle of self-interest. That means that there is such a thing as natural benevolence or at least disinterestedness. I reckon that calls into question the Me First philosophy of your Hobbes and your Mandeville – and blows apart the free-market political philosophy that goes with it. Sympathetic identification is the natural starting point for a radical politics.'

'You mean that we project ourselves into an imaginary future in which we're out of work ourselves and that makes us believe in the welfare state? That strikes me as a defeatist attitude towards ourselves and a weak justification for handing out the money of hard-working taxpayers to welfare scroungers.'

'You're missing the point: it's the capacity for imaginative empathy that's the distinctively human thing. That's what allows us to put ourselves in the position of those less fortunate than we are.'

We argued on, though in increasingly desultory fashion. Elder certainly wasn't going to give way, but at the end of the evening he had the grace to slap his friend on the back and say 'We'll make a philosopher of you yet.' I was glad of the concession, but did not think I wanted to be a philosopher. I just liked kicking around ideas, and found the company of Elder much more rewarding than that of the art students.

[A blank here. Then half-formed memories, half-unburied pain.]

The open page of a philosophy book, but the words mere shapes. No sequence, no meanings, no enlightenment.

Was it something to do with a girl?

Or a friendship betrayed? The island in this sea is but

a single sentence: 'I can't believe you've done this to me.'

«« »»

Laura was annoyed. He always drew back just when it was getting interesting. Had Elder taken a girl off him? And then there was the question of homosexual attraction. If only she could have more time, that would be well worth pursuing.

Although she found William's intellectualizing pompous, his writing held her attention because every now and then something real shone through. It was as if in writing for her, he was reaching out for someone to trust, seeking a new friend, a replacement for his father, for Peggy or Elder. She liked the role.

The trouble with Jack, she thought, was that he just switched off when I talked about my work. He didn't see that the theoretical jargon was a defence. I needed to talk about other people's hang-ups because I couldn't talk about my own. Amanda knows that, but she also knows better than to say so. If only I could find a lover who could also be a sister.

Then she collected herself. 'Come on, Foster, you've got to get through this stuff, just in case *his* defence slips or a new paradigm emerges.' She returned to the page.

«« »»

The student romance, the romance of being a student, such as it had been, had gone sour. 'You need to get away from it all – right now,' Elder had said. 'Go abroad – anywhere,

80

just get out of England – one must risk something in order to do anything.'

My friend was right. I had learnt all I could at art school. Now I had to make my way without a teacher. Or rather, to learn directly from the true masters. I fantasized about the art scene in New York, but there was no possibility of affording the flight, let alone the cost of living there. I would have liked the warmth of Florence, but an exclusive diet of old masters would not have been fresh or healthy. It had to be Paris: cheap to get there on the boat-train, cheap to live there on baguettes and Camembert, the Louvre full of old masters, the Jeu de Paumes of Impressionists, the dealers' shops and little galleries of contemporary work. I had French enough to get by, and could always teach English classes in order to survive.

Calais was a very miserable place in itself, but the remains of the fortifications about it attracted my eye. The walls were much decayed, grown dark-coloured. The country till within a few miles of Paris was flat and uninteresting. My first impression of Paris itself was of dirt and noise, narrow streets and graffiti. I had arranged to rent a room in the rue Coq Héron, a little cut-through street off the rue du Louvre. I arrived after dark and my only sense of the exterior was of an immensely tall building with peeling paintwork. On ascending the scores of murkily lit stairs to my tiny room on the top floor, I fell into bed.

But when I opened the shutters in the morning, the sky was of a much deeper blue than that over London. I smelt the morning bread upon the air and when I went down to the streets they seemed miraculously clean, as if they had been washed and freshened especially for me. I discovered that it took less than ten minutes to walk to the Louvre, past the bustle of the Bourse du Commerce.

Walking from the station the previous day, Paris had cast me down as London had done; I had wondered whether the adventure might not be a huge mistake, whether I would have done better to return to the clear air of Shropshire. But once I came towards the Seine, everything changed. The buildings overlooking the river were glorious, the Louvre above all. This was the place to be. And so began my routine of looking at the paintings in the day, sketching copies, then returning to my little room in the evening and writing down my impressions of both the paintings and the place. Sometimes I varied the walk to or from the museum by taking a street which ran at an angle to the main road; to my delight, it was called the rue Jean-Jacques Rousseau.

The city was a paradox. On bright days it dazzled the eye like a steel mirror, yet it was a vast pile of tall and dirty alleys. The stately, old-fashioned shops and jutting angles of the houses gave it the venerable appearance of antiquity, while the textures and colours to which the eye was constantly drawn made everything seem alive and modern.

You could not dawdle in the streets. You were in danger of being run over every instant. If you weren't looking out the whole time, taxis and vans would come up against you with a sudden acceleration of pace and a thundering noise that dislocated your nervous system till you were brought to yourself by having the same startling process repeated. It seemed that the continual panic in which the pedestrian was kept, the alarm and the escape from it, the anger and the laughter at it, must have had an effect on the Parisian character, and tended to make it the whiffling, skittish, snappish, volatile thing it was.

To improve my French, I read the newspaper each day over breakfast. One morning, under the headline Death of the Author, it reported that a famous essayist had been run over and killed by a laundry van as he stepped forward to cross the street. This confirmed my view of the Paris traffic. Out of curiosity, I dipped into the dead author's writings. I liked his broad range of matter: reading, writing, wrestling, photography, memory, solitude, pleasure, love. I liked the way in which he threw himself into each subject; I was intrigued by, but did not pretend to understand, his claim that all writing is rewriting of what is already written. I wish I could remember his name.

I found it hard to square the Parisians' sophistication with their penchant for small dogs. The citizens' very walk – *the light, jerking, fidgeting trip on which they prided themselves, thinking it grace and spirit* – was in my eyes the effect of the copious heaps of canine excrement over which one was obliged to make one's way on tiptoe, as over a succession of stepping stones, and which rendered natural ease and steadiness out of the question.

On sunny days, I took a long break over lunchtime, justifying it to myself by saying that my eyes hurt with the concentration of copying. I would walk along the *quais*, pausing over the faded brown title-pages of cellophane-wrapped volumes in the coffins of the *bouquinistes*. I would reach the Île de la Cité and sit outside Notre-Dame. I did not like the rearing slab of its façade, preferring the south side, with its seven twin-pillared sentry boxes halfway up the wall, a gargoyle emerging from each, its great rose window with the smaller rose above, and the curve of the flying buttresses. Once, a young man in a leather jacket said to me, 'Vous êtes sportif?', and asked if I wanted to accompany him to the sun. I did not know how literal an offer this was intended to be.

I would cross to the Left Bank and sit in the little park by St-Julien-le-Pauvre. I loved the exterior of the tiny Romanesque church which, I read, had been used for the storage of animal feed during the revolutionary years. But the only time I ventured inside, Mass was in progress and the overpowering smell and the low chant in an unknown language made me slip swiftly out. I hated the scent of orthodoxy, the tyrannical authority of priesthoods.

Stirred by thoughts of revolution, I walked on the Left Bank, overheard snatches of conversation outside Gibert Jeune's bookshop and imagined myself in the class of '68. Looking at the Sorbonne, I became angry as I had not been before that my humble background and provincial school had – so I made myself believe – excluded me from the possibility of attending an ancient university myself.

One showery day I took the metro to the east of the city to the burial ground of Père-Lachaise. I found the elaborate nineteenth-century bourgeois family tombs vulgar in the extreme, tricked out and over-acted as if there were nothing sacred from what the plain Englishman in me regarded as French impertinence and affectation. But I had two pilgrimages to make. One of the paintings to which I had kept returning in the Louvre was Géricault's *Raft of the 'Medusa'*. I could not work out how it packed so much energy into the darkened space of the raft, how the sinister ochre of the sky had been mixed, how the muscles of the figures had been made to ripple and their hands to stretch. Géricault had become one of my heroes. The second tomb I wanted to find was that of Marcel Proust, whom I had been painstakingly reading late at night or when I was woken early by the noises rising from the street. I only managed a few labyrinthine sentences each day, but they were enough to convince me that Proust must be the greatest of all craftsmen of prose and that memory must be the greatest of all literary themes.

I found Proust first. A low rectangular slab of marble in absolute black. Nothing but the name and date chiselled at the foot, the lettering in gold. It is like a book, I thought to myself, a hard and infinitely durable text. I stood alone, silent, bowed in thought. I would never read all the way through to the final recovery of time, but I knew that Proust would be a perpetual companion for the rest of my days.

I worked my way down towards the block of graves where the map at the entrance had told me I would find Géricault. The *Raft* was reproduced in bas-relief; the painter himself lay above it, palette and brush in hand. As I was gazing at the bronze, asking myself how long it would have taken to stain to its pale green, two young men approached. One of them asked, 'Do you know where Jim Morrison is?' I almost replied that I did not know who Jim Morrison was, but that would not have been strictly true. Although I had little interest in rock music, I was vaguely away of the cult surrounding the lead singer of The Doors following his death (drugs? suicide?) in Paris. Not that I felt any sympathy with the cult, as I might have done had it attached itself to a singer whose words I admired – Dylan, say, or Paul Simon. I now remembered that Père-Lachaise was the destination of other young pilgrims besides myself. I said that I was afraid I did not know, but out of curiosity, once I had made my farewell to Géricault, I followed the downhill path the youths had taken. It began to rain.

It was incongruous to see so much long hair, leather and faded denim in a cemetery. About twenty people were gathered round a sandy plot. The adjacent family tombs were covered in graffiti; a broken pillar lay on its side. The grave itself was covered in ash and butts, metro tickets, tattered roses, some still in their cellophane. Cigarettes had been left burning by the headstone like candles before a shrine, joss sticks for incense. The sweet smell of marijuana filled the air. On the top left corner of the grave a girl had placed her passport photo. Another girl, shaking her head and saying quietly, 'C'est trop sale,' was picking up some of the stubs of joints and cigarettes. Groups of two and three came and went. Most stood silently for several minutes, wearing the dazed but fascinated faces of witnesses to a car crash. I could not take my eyes off the graffiti: 'Dan Jez John', 'Come on baby light my PANTS', 'To the poet whose words will never die', 'kill kill kill your enemies', 'Break on through to the other side of reality', 'U R ALIVE', 'Death makes angels of us all and gives us wings for we had shoulders smooth as ravens claws'. No apostrophes, I thought. 'Concession à perpétuité', read the neighbouring grave.

I looked at my fellow pilgrims: they were my generation but they were complete strangers to me. What would they have said if I had told them that my heroes at the age of twenty were Proust and Géricault?

I walked back up the hill. Through the trees I glimpsed

the gold dome of Les Invalides. I thought of Napoleon, the original of all heroes. I remembered how I had thrown myself into arguments with my history teacher at school and with my father: had Napoleon been the sword-arm of the revolution, seeking to carry its ideals across Europe (my own view), or had he been the cause of its extinction, the prototype of the modern dictator (my master's view)?

Then I found myself on the eastern edge of the cemetery. I was not really looking at the graves, but my eye was caught by a small grey cat sitting placidly on a headstone, looking every bit like a funereal monument that had come to life. The grave bore the name of Paul Eluard, which meant nothing to me. I looked more closely; this seemed to be a row of thematically related graves and monuments. To the French volunteers of the International Brigade. In homage to the communist women who gave their lives for the victory of liberty against Nazism, for the triumph of peace. Memorial upon memorial to the *fusillés* of the Resistance and the dead of the Camps. Some words about justice and liberty ascribed to the same Eluard.

A few yards away, there was an old wall bearing a plaque inscribed 'Aux Morts de la Commune 21–28 Mai 1871'. I remembered the Commune from history lessons at school, too. The teacher had explained that it was a last – quixotic? heroic? – attempt to rekindle the original values of the revolution, snuffed out in a hail of rifle fire at the end of May. But perhaps it was not the last. Those volunteers who had gone to Spain, these heroes of the Resistance – were they not fighting for the three words carved on all the great public buildings in Paris?

I remembered then that in 1968 my father had spoken

those three words – *liberté, égalité, fraternité* – like a mantra. I felt in my blood the truth of other words which I had never previously understood: idealism, sacrifice, hope. I thought of my argument with Elder. My friend would have pointed to the *Raft of the 'Medusa'* and said that when the going gets rough the spirit of self-preservation will lead us to eat each other. I would not have replied; I would have walked Elder to this part of the graveyard and stood in silent humility.

I had surprised myself. I had come to make a youthful gesture of homage to two artistic heroes – on reflection, I realized that in this I was no different from those I had scorned a quarter of an hour before. Now I was crying with pride and thankfulness for the example of thousands of unknown men and women. I looked through my tears and saw that the place of the heroic dead was alive with feral cats, moving gracefully, purposefully.

That night I sat in my room with the blank page of my notebook. All I could think of was a single phrase: 'As if the spirits of the freedom fighters were quick'. I wondered where the cats went at night.

As the months went by, my writing about the paintings and about Paris came to mean more to me than the sketching. Rapid sketching suited me best, but each day I discovered that, after the first hour or two, I generally made my pictures worse and worse, the more pains I took with them. The written sketches, on the other hand, the pen portraits of paintings and people and places, flowed on. My instincts told me that I would never make a painter. But in Paris I found that I might be a writer. I had no idea whether I would ever make a living as one, but I was capable of writing some things that satisfied me more than any of my paintings had ever done. Whether in my little room seeing only the roofs and the sky, or sitting with a notebook in a café stretching out the length of a simple meal or making a single *infusion* last more than an hour, it was the writing that proved itself my therapy.

From then on, what mattered about the paintings I saw was not so much the technique to be learnt from them as the way they made me see the world. It was almost as if the attempt to gain technical mastery had stood between me and the true purpose of looking at a painting. Art school, with its life classes that were dead to life, its ramshackle juxta-positions of indulgent abstraction with tedious minutiae of shading and brushwork, suddenly seemed an imposition, a wrong turning, a wasted year. My first entrance into the Louvre had not been a mere event in my journey, as it was for the thousands of tourists who surrounded me: *it was an event in my life, remembered ever after with thankfulness and regret.* Thankfulness for the worlds to which it opened my eyes, regret for the knowledge that I could no longer fancy saying with Correggio, 'I also am a painter.'

Every object in Paris became lustrous from the light thrown back upon it by the mirror of art. The painters were teaching me to look at nature with different eyes. Through their grace, I began to understand the texture and meaning of the visible universe, to see into the life of things. When I walked in the Tuileries gardens on a sunny Sunday after-noon, the milling crowd basked in the glow and flow of the paint with which Pissarro had caught their grandparents. Children with rods pushed toy boats towards the centre of a large round pond; caught in the light breeze, the boats wheeled and turned and their sails took bright colours from Monet and Seurat.

The Tuileries gardens and *The Man in Black* by Titian in the Louvre close by ('whose features,' I wrote ponderously in my notebook, 'form a sombre pendant to the light parterres') were the two things in Paris I liked best. 'I shall never tire,' I scribbled more lightly, 'of walking in the one, and of looking at the other.'

In afterlife, I marked the epoch in one of my magazine pieces.

It is now fifteen years since I was studying in the Louvre (and I have long since given up all thoughts of painting as a profession), but long after I returned to England, and even still, I sometimes dream of being there again, of asking for the old pictures – and not finding them, or finding them changed or faded from what they were, I cry myself awake.

10

Laura decided that William was rather like herself. Perhaps that was why she rather liked him, despite herself. He kept introducing technicalities – all this jargon about art – as defences against emotion. But at the same time he treasured his memories.

The thing she liked about his writing was its way of bringing back memories of her own. Reading about his time in Paris, she kept thinking about her summer in San Francisco in her student days. She could not get the smells of the Chinese quarter out of her head. She felt warm inside.

But what could be done therapeutically with this empathy between writer and reader? She read on.

«« »»

When I ran out of money I returned to England. I overheard a conversation on the cross-channel ferry. One of the passengers was talking about a man who had courted a woman for thirteen years before marrying her. 'Then at least,' said a fellow Englishman, 'he'd have a good idea of her character.' A Frenchman replied, 'No, not at all – the very next day she might turn out to be the very reverse of the character that she had appeared to be during all the preceding time.' I thought that the Frenchman was right, but said nothing.

Back in London, I at first slept on the floor in my

brother's cramped apartment, then, thanks to a modest commission which my brother passed on to me, rented a room of my own that was even tinier than the one in Paris. Although my heart was no longer in my painting, I managed to fulfil the commission and a second one which followed from it. John was completing a portrait of a prominent businessman, commissioned to hang in the company board-room, when he had been approached to undertake a copy in oils from a colour photograph which a man wanted at short notice as an anniversary present for his wife. Since he did not have time to do even the crude job that would have sufficed, he gave the work to me. In truth, he probably also saw the opportunity to set his brother on his financial feet as a way of getting him off his own floor.

The couple liked the painting so much that they recommended me to some friends, who decided they would 'do it properly' and sit for a pair of portraits. Could they come in to the artist's studio? Not having a studio, and having imposed enough on my brother, I hastily replied that I preferred to see my subjects in the atmosphere of their own home, where they were always more relaxed. It had the added advantage that some favourite *objet* could be included in the picture.

I knew that I had done serviceable work and that my close study of the masters had saved me from many of the pitfalls into which modern portrait-painters often fall. ('The wrinkles in Rembrandt are not hard lines,' I had scribbled in my Paris notebook, 'but broken and irregular.') But I was dissatisfied. Once I had copied some of Titian's por-traits in the Louvre, my ambitions had flown absurdly high.

Nothing would serve my turn save heads like Titian – Titian expressions, Titian complexions, Titian dresses, the cat-like watchfulness of Titian eyes. These were not to be found among the London *nouveaux riches* who were the only people likely to commission work from an unknown young artist. So after one or two abortive attempts to engraft Renaissance Italian art on to modern English nature, I flung away my pencil in disgust and despair. *I might have been no worse a painter than any, but gave up the attempt out of a desire to do too well.*

I had no desire to be rich. There was, I believed, an essential difference of character in mankind between those who wished *to do* and those who wished *to have*. Increasingly through my twenties, I observed people expressing the strongest desire to possess fine houses, cars, clothes, and the strongest envy of those who had them.

I myself had no such feeling, nor the least ambition to shine except by doing something better than others. I had the love of power, but not of property. I would have liked to be able to outstrip a racehorse in speed, but I would have been ashamed to take any merit to myself from possessing the fastest racehorse in the world. It was a time in which people seemed to be estimated by what they possessed instead of what they were, but I knew that I could not transfer my personal identity from myself to what I merely called mine.

[Laura, I'm writing this in the night. Can't see the page clearly, but can't stop the memories coming. Hope you can read it.]

I had to make a living, but it wouldn't be as a mediocre

portrait painter. For a time, I had a job restocking the shelves in an off-licence.

In my lunch hour I would sit with a sandwich and a book in a corner of the basement where the cases of wine were stored. Certain books would always bring back the smell of cardboard and the stale, vinegary odour of spillages that had not been properly mopped up. My arms ached from the weight of the dozen-bottle boxes, and in the evenings I was usually too tired to read any more or to write. I looked at my Paris notebooks and word sketches, but lacked the energy to work them into anything publishable.

Then, suddenly, I was galvanized. Since my return from Paris, I had seen very little of Elder. But one day I returned from work to find a scribbled note saying, 'Open lecture tonight – could be up your street. Meet me in Union bar, 7.30. A.E.' Tired as I was, I made myself go. Elder, who was now a graduate student, explained that the speaker had been snubbed by the university many years ago – been denied tenure or promotion or something – and had gone to teach abroad. He rarely acceded to invitations to lecture in England, but since this one had come from the students' union he had accepted it in the knowledge that there would be a far bigger turnout for him than there ever was for the second-rate minds who had achieved tenure and who week by week gave the university's dull, parochial, officially sanctioned lectures.

Elder was right. The Union common room was packed when we squeezed our way in at ten to eight. By the time the lecture was due to begin, students were perched on the windowsills, standing at the back, sitting on the floor at the front literally at the feet of the master. He entered to a buzz of anticipation, a short, stockily built man with dark hair, one arm held awkwardly, almost as if he were trying to hide it.

The introduction was botched by the president of the student literary society, who was doubtless overawed by the size of the audience (Elder explained in a stage whisper that meetings usually consisted of no more than a dozen aficionados listening to readings by poets whose sole publications were slim volumes from private presses of legendary obscurity). The title of the lecture was announced as the Act of Reading. The lights were dimmed and a projector was switched on.

The image that was projected on to the tall white screen at the front of the room remained there throughout the hour. The lecturer was thus caught in a kind of half-light, illuminated from behind his right shoulder by the brightness reflected off the screen. He spoke without a lectern, without notes. He seemed more comfortable with his body in partial shadow, his face sometimes catching the direct beam of the projector light. *His forehead was broad and high, light as if built of ivory, with large projecting eyebrows, and his eyes rolling beneath them, like a sea with darkened lustre.* Yet as he spoke, or rather rolled out his discourse, a twinkle sometimes seemed to be detectable in the eye – it said, Challenge me if you dare, call me a charlatan and a word conjurer and let us fight it out between us. Just remember that I have read more books than you have – all of them in their original language.

When the image was projected on to the screen, I almost fell off my chair. It was a painting that I had studied for hours in the Louvre. A middle-aged man was bent over a large book. He wore an expression of complete absorption. In his left hand he held the page he had just turned; his right arm rested solidly on the book. Three other books were to be seen beside him, two standing upright, one lying flat. Their position and their colours seemed to echo the posture of the reader and the colours in his robe and hat, as if to suggest he was a man with a peculiar affinity for books. On his green baize desktop there was an hourglass and a quill in an inkwell. There were also three large coins. I remembered having puzzled over these when I first looked at the painting: were they symbols which said that books were things of great value or were we supposed to imagine that they were like Roman medallions commemorating great men? The room in which the reader sat had an almost monastic austerity. The wall at the back was of large, cold blocks of stone. I had liked the painting and felt quite pleased with my pencilled copy of it. There had been something approachable about it: it was in the style of my revered Rembrandt, but less sublime, more everyday and for that reason less inimitable.

I had not worked out the significance of what seemed to be a collection of flasks and containers on a high shelf at the back. I now learnt that the painting was originally called *The Chemist in his Laboratory*, although the figure was that of the fellow artist who had initiated the painter in the work of Rembrandt. When it was exhibited for a second time, however, it was retitled *A Philosopher Engaged in his Reading*. Painter, chemist, philosopher: all were subsumed under the category of Reader. That, the lecturer said, was the point of the painting. In Enlightenment culture, the man engaged in the act of reading is the embodiment of civilization.

The lecturer's range of reference was astounding. The thrust of his argument was that reading was once truly an *act* but now it was degenerating, dying. For centuries it had been a sacred action. The subject of the painting had *dressed* to read, not merely as one might dress for dinner but as a priest would robe himself before performing the sacrament. The study in which the act took place would be silent, whereas young people now read with music blaring or the television jabbering. The book on the table had a texture worthy of its content; it was no flimsy paperback. Here a quotation from an essay by someone called Walter Benjamin on the subject of unpacking his library, together with a lament that modern apartments had no room for sturdy bookshelves.

The reader had his quill to emend, annotate and transcribe the text. His coins were a symbolic reminder that words outlive brass. And thus each detail in the painting became the starting point for a spiralling discourse on the mind of Europe: the hourglass led to a brief history of time, to Ovid's *Tempus edax rerum* and to Shakespeare, to Poussin's *Et in Arcadia ego* and the internal exile of Osip Mandelstam; the coins on the table to the house of fame, to Scaliger on medallions and the orations of Demosthenes. Names and quotations dropped like dew – Montaigne in his tower and Yeats in his, Pound in his cage and Heidegger at Todtnauberg where Celan visited him to ask Adorno's unanswerable question. Cabbalists jostled with humanists with *philosophes*, the adages of Erasmus with the aphorism of Benjamin (that name again) that there was no document of civilization which was not also a document of barbarism. The encyclopaedic enterprise of D'Alembert and Diderot had been replaced by the nausea of Sartre and the *ennui* of Musil. The west was in decline because the act of reading had been dying around us ever since the advent of mass culture – a passing remark, half-respectful, half-sneering, about one of the few English figures to be mentioned in the lecture, F. R. Leavis (at last a name familiar to me, for Leavis had been my English teacher's tutor). There had been only two voices in our low, dishonest century which had spoken with sufficient power of the need to restore the aura to the act. Benjamin's was one, the other was that of the later Heidegger, who had understood that in the work of art is to be found the original admission of dwelling, the authentic thinking of being. *In digressing, in dilating, in passing from subject to subject, the lecturer appeared to float in air, to slide on ice.*

I was mesmerized. I understood but a tenth of what was said, but I knew that vast worlds were being opened to me. The lecturer had a knack of making every writer he quoted sound fascinating, all-important, the holder of the key to all mythologies. One moment I would be thinking that I must go out first thing in the morning and buy the complete essays of Montaigne, the next I would determine to work my way through Musil's *roman-fleuve*. Every sentence was perfectly turned, every point was made with fierce conviction, as if the future of the world depended upon it. There was no subject on which the lecture did not touch, none on which it rested; it would plunge deep into hermeneutics, pluck from a vacuum some monument of unageing intellect, then return to the dizzying heights of the Italian Renaissance or the French Enlightenment. The professor's piercing eye twinkled in the projector beam, motes of dust playing around it, as he dilated on the brevity of life and the corridors full of books one would never have time to read. 'Yesterday in the library my eye fell upon Sarpi's *History of the Council of Trent*,' he remarked as if from the blue, and he was in flight again, passing to me the flame of curiosity and the cloak of reverence.

As we made our way out, I asked Elder if he had been similarly inspired. 'Pure hokum, old boy – these continental types don't know what a real philosophical argument is. What they need is a cold dose of logical positivism, the hard edge of the Anglo-American analytical tradition. That would put a stop to all their windy rhetoric. I've just spotted a couple of friends – do you want to join us for a drink?'

I declined. I had been able to keep up with Elder's undergraduate studies of the traditional philosophical questions, but what my friend was now talking about was a closed book I had no desire to open. And I certainly did not want to be in the company of anyone who had reacted to the lecture with cynicism. I was glad to be with myself, alone.

On my way back to my little room that night I had a sound in my ears: it was the voice of the sage. I had a light before me: it was the knowledge that I would be a writer. The lecture had to me *something of the effect that arises from the turning up of fresh soil or of the first welcome breath of spring.*

As, in the dim hours of this hospital night, I remember the night of the lecture, I hear again the voice which told of the feeling of immortality in youth:

I was at that time dumb, inarticulate, helpless, but now my ideas float on winged words, and as they expand their plumes, catch the golden light of other years. My soul has indeed remained in its original bondage, dark, obscure, with longings infinite and unsatisfied; my heart, shut up in the prison-house of this rude clay, has never found, nor will it ever find, a heart to speak to; but that my understanding also did not remain dumb and brutish, or at length found a language to express itself, I owe to him.

But still I have no access to the name of the lecturer. And thinking back over it again, I am not even sure whether it was a lecture or a sermon.

11

Now Laura was losing interest. All these books, names of dead writers and philosophers. When William had been remembering Paris, she had become excited by the writing cure, had fleetingly wondered if she might develop it as a new form of special treatment. It had the great advantage over the talking cure that patients could get on with it on their own. Psychotherapy's problem had always been the twenty-three hours of the day not spent in the consulting room. But, just as there were always long periods of evasion and circumlocution during each fifty-minute conversation in the room, so she would have to accept that there would be many pages of writing in which nothing significant would be revealed.

Although the story of the lecture had not interested her, she granted that William had remembered it with a passion which she could not help admiring. Amanda had that kind of passion for her books and authors. Laura felt that William's memory had been refined by the night. Glancing through the remaining pages, she detected a cooling of intensity. She attributed this not only to the exteriority of the subject matter, but also to the fact that he was writing in the morning. She wondered what it would be like to conduct a therapeutic conversation at three o'clock in the morning.

Then she told herself to keep alert. You never knew when the next breakthrough was going to come.

«« »»

[Morning.]

Over the next few weeks every minute of free time was devoted to writing. To begin with, I had no idea what direction to take. All I knew was that I wanted words to flow from my pen as they had spilt from the tongue of the exiled professor.

I thought back on my discussions with Elder about self-interest against empathetic power, and started an essay on the subject. But I soon put it aside as being too abstruse. If I had one criticism of the professor, it was the inaccessibility of some of his ideas, the Olympian tone of speaking *de haut en bas*. I wanted to make important ideas and great art available to all. The political ideals I had inherited from my father had a lot to do with this. The arts should belong to the people; the world of reading should be a republic, not an aristocracy. You didn't need to put on a fine robe or possess an original edition to take nourishment from a book. I tried writing my own essay: on not the *act* of reading but the *pleasure* of it.

I was initially quite pleased with what I found myself saying about the pleasures of *re*-reading. In my late teens, my favourite novel had been *Tom Jones*. I had read it over and over again; I believed I almost knew it by heart.

In turning to a well-known author, there is not only an assurance that our time will not be thrown away, but we also have the pleasure of shaking hands with, and looking in the face of, an old, tried and valued friend. We compare notes and chat the hours away. We form dear friendships with such ideal guests, dearer perhaps and more lasting than those with our most intimate acquaintance. In reading a book which is an old favourite with me (say the first novel I ever adored) I not only have the pleasure of imagination and of a critical relish of the work, but the pleasures of memory added to it. It recalls the same feelings and associations which I had in first reading it, and which I can never have again in any other way. Associations of this kind are links in the chain of our conscious being. They bind together the different scattered divisions of our personal identity. They are landmarks and guides in our journey through life. They are pegs and loops on which we can hang up, and from which we can take down at our pleasure, the wardrobe of a moral imagination, the relics of our best affections, the tokens and records of our happiest hours.

But on re-reading my disquisition on re-reading, I lost faith in it. No one else I knew regarded their books as their closest friends; no one would understand. And there was no obvious forum in which to publish reflections of this sort.

Next I tried to write up my sketches of Parisian life, turning them into a piece which I could offer to the travel pages of a magazine. I began: 'The rule for travelling abroad is to take our common sense with us and leave our prejudices behind us.' I gave as an example of prejudice the English tendency to describe the French as like monkeys merely because they gesticulated constantly with rapid arm-movements. But on re-reading this I felt it had too much aphorism, anecdote and atmosphere, not enough practical advice to be appropriate.

I persevered. On further reflection, it seemed to me that

my best chance of getting a first break – and I convinced myself that once I had made the breakthrough, my future would be assured – was to stay within the bounds of what I knew. I wrote an article called 'On first visiting the Louvre', in which I sought to convey something of the magic of the place whilst also guiding my reader through its labyrinthine corridors towards a handful of works which, I said, they *had* to see on their first visit. I explained that to look properly at all the paintings in the Louvre would take a lifetime – I had been there daily for months and had but begun my journey along the corridors – but that, provided specific objectives were set, one could gain tremendous profit and pleasure from a single visit of some three to four hours. In selecting my recommendations, I omitted the *Mona Lisa* altogether and mixed well-known works such as *The Raft of the 'Medusa'* with comparatively obscure ones such as Chardin's portrait of his master, Joseph Aved.

I included a Titian of course, and wrote of it, copying from notes I had made when I stood in front of it, 'Not only does the head seem to think – the body seems to feel.'

I was not afraid to pass judgement on my masters.

Poussin succeeded better in classic than in sacred subjects. The latter are comparatively heavy, forced full of violent contrasts of colour, of red, blue and black, and without the sense of the prophetic which the characters ought to inspire. But who, on the other hand, could sufficiently praise his picture of the shepherds in the vale of Tempe going out on a fine morning of the spring and coming to a tomb with the inscription 'Et in Arcadia ego'? The eager curiosity of some, the expression of others who start back with fear and surprise, the clear breeze playing with the branches of the shadowing trees, the distant, uninterrupted, sunny prospect speak (and for ever will speak on) of ages past to ages yet to come.

I wrote of general feelings as well as particular paintings:

'What is it about visiting art galleries that moves us so? Is it the coming close to the very texture of the paint as we press forward to the canvas to read the brushstrokes, then step back to take in the whole? Or is it the glimpse of the many lives enacted in the paintings? Our pleasure in painting is a manifestation of that empathetic imaginative power which marks our humanity.'

The article was accepted by the first editor to whom I submitted it. It was a little highbrow, but the magazine was planning a special two-part supplement on weekend breaks in Paris and a touch of class would not go amiss. Not only would they run my piece (re-titling it 'Highlights of the Louvre'), they also asked for a sequel, to go in the second part, 'Highlights of the Jeu de Paume.'

Again, I mixed the celebrated with the less known: of Manet, *Le Déjeuner sur l'Herbe*; of Cézanne, not the card players but the view of the Gulf of Marseille from L'Estaque. Its aquamarine and terracotta rendering of pellucid Mediterranean light; the few boats. What fascinated me about this painting were its lines, which somehow seemed to give spatial representation to my own conception of the lines that ran between mind and world. You could see a lane winding down towards the sea, which suggested our normal course into a landscape, but every now and then you would look at the painting and the protruding chimney in the foreground would become a straight road heading for the water – this was like the sudden, hyper-real, pure vision of a memory spot (which would vanish when you noticed the black smudge of the chimney's tip). And then the spit stretching into the water on the far side of the gulf would carry the eye to the hazier blue of the hills beyond, their distance being like that of childhood.

I could not begin to explain this in my article. Instead, I copied my more general thoughts on Cézanne from my notebook.

As the objects themselves in nature would produce an impression on the sense, distinct from every other object, and having something in it which the heart owns and the imagination consecrates, the objects in the picture preserve the same impression, absolute, unimpaired, stamped with all the truth of passion and the joy of sight.

The art of Cézanne (somewhat surprisingly, my father's favourite painter) was, I said, characterized by an *intensity* which allowed for a unique fusion of the object and the subject, nature and the self:

'Everything in every one of his landscapes is there for a reason. In whatever he does there is a significance, a consciousness beyond any other painter. He stands on the cusp between tradition and modernity, representation and abstraction. He understands the relationship between the form of things and the emotions they inspire.'

I went on to argue against the grain of the formalism in which I had been trained at art school:

'The Impressionists matter to us not because of their brushwork, their innovative effects of light, but because they offer us narratives of ordinary life. Their shimmer is like that of the memory – they conjure up images from our own earlier lives. Sunday outings and picnics when we were children; city, park and riverbank.'

When I saw my words set in type, I felt a thrill and a sadness. Print conferred an authority and a permanence upon what had previously been my fugitive thoughts and jottings. But whatever I published from now on, there would never again be the shiver down the spine which I sensed on this first meeting with the published self who was and was not my own self.

When my payment arrived, it seemed like untold riches. I gave up the job at the off-licence. Now I could call myself a professional freelance writer.

«« »»

On the last page there was a postscript addressed directly to Laura.

«« »»

Laura, I've been writing almost constantly since I left your office. Guess the chemical thing won't be necessary – it didn't sound like your style.

We must be nearly there. Just a few more days. If I could only remember a few practical details, I would be able to confirm my name and trace myself – addresses, national insurance number. The name of the magazine, the date of the two articles – some time in the early 1980s is as far as I can get.

But perhaps I should not be worrying about the practicalities. They can come later. In its way it is liberating to have no known address, not to be an insurance number or a face on an identity card. What matters is that I am beginning to piece together my history, to discover the kind of person I am. I am filling the ruled pad, emptying the cartridges of ink. The memories are beginning to flow more sequentially.

There are, however, still gaps. The blank months towards the end of the year at art school. I read the name Sally on a nurse's lapel and there was one of those gleams of light, as when the man in the next bed had said William. But, hard as I worked to create a picture of Sally, none came.

Is my mind blocking something deliberately? Looking back over the pages I have filled, I am struck that it is my work I am remembering. That other self, the William on the printed page, is speaking to me. His words are alive, whereas my own emotional life remains dead. I still need your help for that.

12

She broke her rule and spoke first.

'William, I'm interested in what you've been writing and if I had the time I'd be very happy to talk to you about it. But this is a hospital, not a writing school. You're no longer suffering any physical effects from your fall. We've recovered a lot of information about your past – if it is your past. The only thing preventing me from discharging you immediately is that you haven't given us a name and address. I can't discount the possibility that for some reason you're deliberately withholding them from me.'

She waited for a reaction.

When he said 'I'm not', she felt inclined to believe him. He might be able to act with his eyes closed, feigning hypnosis. He could fabricate anything he wished on paper. But she was convinced that face-to-face in a therapeutic encounter she always knew when someone was telling a direct lie. There were liars who blinked or looked away; there were liars who fixed her with their eyes and barely blinked at all; and then there were eyes in which she read evasion but not downright deceit. William had eyes of the third kind.

'Then what I recommend is this. You say that you're a writer. I can discharge you. Then you can go to the library in Edinburgh and find your past writings. Go through the back numbers of the magazines – you'll find yourself there, won't you?'

He said, 'I'm not sure it will work. I know that William's a writer, but I don't know for sure that I'm him. I mean, I may not be that William. And if I'm not, then we know precisely zilch about who I am. How can you discharge me if that's the case? Besides, where would I go, what would I live on? I didn't have any money when I was found.'

She explained the system: a temporary social security number, signing on the register of unemployed, dole money, housing the responsibility of the local authority. It was for him to decide whether he would stay near the hospital or go into Edinburgh or return to England. He would be entitled to some out-patient consultations. If he stayed in the area, she could try to fit him in herself.

She allowed the prospect to sink in. She could tell from his eyes that the attempt to make him panic was working.

'Let me tell you my dream,' he said.

She looked sceptical, as if to say, You must have a pretty low opinion of me if you think you can get out of this with some Freudian caricature like your seven-inch conversation.

But before she could speak, he launched into the dream, explaining it was the first he'd had – or at least the first he'd remembered – since the accident.

'I could feel the beads of sweat on my forehead. I was twitching from the dream, breathless. I was dead. I'd been killed by my lover's scorn. It wasn't clear how she'd killed me – perhaps I'd been driven to suicide, perhaps I'd simply done away with the will to live, stopped eating and walked into oblivion. I was a ghost. I was in a bedroom, watching.

Conversations

The room was similar to the one in which I had lived and loved, but it wasn't the same room. Her new lover was lying back, drained, limp. She was awake, smiling to herself. Her long flank, dark hair, small breasts. Then she saw me. "But you're dead?" I tried to speak, but couldn't because I was dead. She began to panic. She turned to her lover, whose eyes were closed. "Tommy," she whispered urgently. But he was asleep. "Tommy," again without a response. And my ghostly self smiled, for I knew that Tommy was not asleep but feigning sleep because he thought that he was being called upon to perform yet again. The girl, whose body was pale anyway, was now white, as much of a ghost as I was. Lying bathed in a cold quicksilver sweat. And then by one of dreaming's sudden film-like cuts, I was the man in the bed, lying back, spent. I was telling the girl about the future situation I had just dreamed: how she would kill me by her scorn and my ghost would come to her as she lay with some new lover.'

He paused. He had won back Laura's interest. She asked him if he remembered the dialogue with the girl.

'Yes,' he said, 'it went like this.' The photographic memory was working.

Girl: And what will you say to me?
William: I'm not going to tell you now, because if I did, it wouldn't have any effect on you then.
Girl: You've got a sick sense of humour.
William: I'm not joking.
Girl: Stop it, you're scaring me.
William: You're the one who has the power to stop it, Sarah. All you have to do is remain faithful to me.
Girl: We'll see about that.

'And then she grinned, ugly as she'd never been before, and I awoke, bathed in my own cold quicksilver sweat. I keep trying to bring back the image of the woman in the dream. Because her name was Sarah.'

Laura knew at this moment that she did not want to discharge William – if William he was – until she had heard some more about Sarah. She wanted to find out what sort of woman it was who could place this man under her spell.

She asked if the dream had unlocked anything more specific. Nothing, he said, save that he was convinced to the bottom of his heart that this was the Sarah to whom he had been calling in the nights of his fever.

She asked him if she thought it was significant that the dream involved a sexual rival.

He replied that he had taken a walk in the hospital grounds between breakfast and their appointment. On his walk, he had thought about the dream. He had then remembered a sexual encounter.

'Would you feel comfortable describing it?' asked Laura.

'On the couch I would.'

She allowed him to repeat the previous session's performance, vowing that this would be the last time. This time he did not need the prompting of her quasi-hypnotic patter. He launched into his account, speaking rapidly, jauntily, leaving Laura no opportunity to intervene and invite reflection. Once again, she found herself listening to a story, letting him set the pace.

'I liked the formula of what I'd written about the Paris galleries – its combination of aesthetic reflection with journalistic practicality. I also felt that I owed myself a treat. It had been a long time since I'd seen my family, so I took the train to Shropshire and stayed with my parents for a week. From there, I went on to the Lake District. I'd decided to write a piece on its literary associations. Like the articles on the Paris galleries, it would be aimed at the cultured weekend-breaker. Where before I'd told my readers of key paintings, now I'd describe some notable houses: Dove Cottage, of course, but also Rydal Mount where Wordsworth moved in his more prosperous years, Nab Cottage – that was the home of De Quincey the Opium Eater – and John Ruskin's Brantwood. Oh yes, Beatrix Potter's house too. To give it popular appeal.

'I booked into a cosy family-run hotel in the centre of Grasmere, deciding to give myself three days – the first to research the Wordsworthian associations of the immediate vicinity, then one for Ruskin and Potter, provided the bus times worked out, and the third to take an all-day walk in the hills. The first day went according to plan. On the second I awoke to a cloudless sky. I studied the bus timetable over the magnificent Cumberland sausage I was brought for breakfast. It wasn't going to be possible to visit both the Ruskin and the Potter houses in a single day. I couldn't allow myself to afford an extra night in the hotel, but I didn't want to waste time waiting around for buses on both remaining days. Ruskin would have to be dropped – no matter, nobody was interested in him any more. The important thing was to get in the walk while the weather held.

'Straight after breakfast I was off over Silver How, into the Langdale valley. By lunchtime I was striding up the Band, by mid-afternoon I had conquered Bow Fell and was looking at my map to work out a route back to Grasmere that didn't involve retracing my steps. I slogged across to Serjeant Man and then with renewed energy bounded down to flop on the grass by the gentle lap of Easedale Tarn. I got back to the hotel just on the dinner hour, flushed and triumphant from my eighteen miles of ground and more than five thousand feet of ascent.'

Laura interrupted: 'Maybe the Tourist Board details could be saved for your writing?'

William said that the atmosphere was important. He had to tell it in his own way.

'I'm coming to it,' he went on. 'Deeply contented despite my aching calves, I sat through the evening in the corner of the little bar at the back of the hotel, very slowly sipping down three pints of bitter shandy. I didn't usually trust myself to drink, but I'd earned an exemption. The sweet and bitter taste. The hotel was quiet; the proprietor and his wife had gone into Ambleside for the evening, leaving their daughter behind the bar. By half past ten, I was the only person left. The girl had flicked through her father's tabloid paper. She'd picked up and put down her *Cosmo* a dozen times. She started asking me questions. I answered politely, not really listening. My mind was still out on the fells. The pastoral calm of Langdale; the rearing of Crinkle Crags; from the top, a breathtaking view across to the Scafells. There I go composing the magazine article again.

'Gradually the girl won my attention. Her name was Rose. She was funny, cutting, down-to-earth. She was not impressed that I was a writer. Without intending to, I found myself explaining my dilemma about the bus times. She said that she'd take me to both houses in the car. She hadn't heard of Ruskin, but as a kid she'd liked Beatrix Potter;

she'd always meant to go over to the writer's hilltop home near Hawkshead. They were supposed to have the original drawings there.

'Then her father came in. "Everything all right, love?" She didn't tell him about the arrangement. I excused myself and went to bed.

'The next day it rained. I spent the morning in the guest sitting room, writing up my notes about Wordsworth and Co. The material was all rather dry. Too *sober*. I needed more anecdotes to liven it up – all I had found so far was a passing reference to some young critic of the day who came to Grasmere to pay homage to Wordsworth but was run out of town by the locals because he made a pass at a village girl.

'Rose came in to make up a fire and said she'd be free by twelve. I offered to buy her a pub lunch on the way, to thank her for the ride. She drank vodka and lime – "No, I better not have a third or you'll have to drive." "I can't drive." "You're joking." "I like trains and walking." She explained that she'd just left school and was taking a year out, deciding whether to apply to college or go abroad and make use of her A-level French.

'She liked the Potter illustrations, but we didn't find much else to talk about until we were going round Brantwood. "It's so fucking gloomy," said Rose. "It gives me the creeps." I had been reading up on Ruskin. I had an explanation for the pallor, the air of sterility, which hung around the house, and which was exacerbated by the rain – the place might've felt different on a sunny day, when you could have looked out through the bow window at the glistening surface of Coniston Water.

'"Ruskin was always unfulfilled," I pontificated. "He was so disgusted on his wedding night by the sight of his wife's copious pubic hair that he never consummated the marriage. His expectations of female nudity must have come from his study of the Renaissance – and painters like Titian pretended that there was no such thing as body hair. Then in his later years he became obsessed with an unobtainable young girl called Rose La Touche. I guess what he yearned for was a body too young to be tainted by pubic growth."

'"Yeah, that picture downstairs made him look like a dirty old man," said Rose. I was pedantic: "Well, she was only ten when he first saw her, but I wouldn't say his interest was strictly paedophiliac. Something a little more idealizing than that." She was herself: "You can always dress it up in fancy language."

'I explained that in her teens the girl did grow to love Ruskin, even though he was thirty years older than her. That he must have been a father figure to her. "Did they get it together, then?" "No," I replied. "Her family kept her away from Ruskin, she had a string of nervous breakdowns and died young."

'Then with a grin my companion said, "So since old Ruskin couldn't *touche la rose*, he moved into this godforsaken place?" I was still pontificating: "Yes, he incarcerated himself here and wrote gloomy, prophetic essays about the decline of the times. His obsession with Rose La Touche lasted for years, drove him mad."

'Then she said, in the voice of a child: "I'm Rose, why don't you try touching me?" She winked and scampered downstairs. I followed, mildly shocked, but, I had to admit, rather turned on. The coincidence of names had not occurred to me. We glanced at each other several times in the car on the way back to Grasmere.

'The bar was busier that evening. I drank whisky, justifying it to myself on the grounds of the damp, though in fact the Lake District weather had executed a characteristic U-turn and it had been a glorious evening. Rose came over to me just before eleven. The locals were leaving and most of the guests had gone to their rooms. She said that her father didn't need her any more. What about a walk round the lake? A final bit of research for my article. Wordsworth and that lot were probably always going for midnight walks.

'I went to fetch my coat; she was waiting for me in the lobby, wearing a baggy sweater. There was a chill in the air from the day's rain, but it was a clear night. We walked in silence along the winding lane. I heard a car coming towards us. I grabbed Rose's hand and pulled her in beside the drystone wall. The car headlights dazzled for a moment. "It's narrow, isn't it? Better go carefully." I didn't let go of her hand. A large hand, I thought. Rose was big-boned.

'We stopped by a gate, from where we could see the lake. The surface shone beneath the moon. My eyes had grown used to the pale light. I could see a few shadowy, yellowish sheep in the field between the road and the water. I felt light-headed from the whisky. Rose was wearing a loose, rather shapeless dress beneath the sweater. I was behind her as she leant on the gate. Without thinking about it, I put my hand up the dress. "You don't waste any time," she said. "You told me to touch the rose," I replied.

'We climbed over the gate. I laid my Barbour on the wet

grass and thought for an instant of Sir Walter Ralegh. Her jersey was off already. She stuffed her knickers into the pocket of her dress, then lifted it off over her head. Her strong tongue was hoovering my teeth and gums. Her hands were pulling up my shirt, scraping the skin of my back, unbuckling my belt. I didn't like the texture of her cropped hair. My trousers were round my ankles; I was standing at full mast, her hand clasping me. Save for the whisky, her touch would have burst me immediately. Then I was on top of her. How undignified we must have looked, I thought: her knees bent up towards the mountains, my white buttocks in the moonlight, my socks and shoes still on. But the sheep seemed unperturbed; I could hear the sound of their grass-munching.

'I asked if it was safe. "Just don't go too deep or you might catch yourself on my coil." Had I been sober, the image would have killed my desire. But I wasn't really listening. I was an animal now, needing only to unload. Five, six thrusts were all it took. I apologized: "Not much fun for you." "Don't worry, it was worth it for the sight of your knob sticking up as you stood there with the sheep all around."

'I was relieved that it was too wet to remain on the ground. We walked back, not holding hands this time. All the lights were off in the hotel. Rose unlocked the front door. Before I had a chance to deliver the abashed goodbye I'd been preparing as we walked, she was pulling me into the guest sitting room. She didn't turn the light on. She was peeling off her dress again. "Are you sure it's safe?" I asked lamely, "Suppose your father . . ."

'"You owe me," she replied intransigently. "This time it's for me, so nice and slow – and I want you naked." I realized that there was no choice but to oblige. She licked me into a serviceable erection, then turned on her side and said, "I prefer it from behind." It wasn't a position I was accustomed to; the novelty excited me, but I made myself slow down. All hell would break loose if I didn't wait for her this time. She was beginning to quiver, but I could tell that there was still some way to go. I tried to take my mind off it by thinking of my article. But the image of Ruskin and Rose La Touche only excited me more. I recited other names to myself instead: Peter Rabbit, Jeremy Fisher, Mrs Tiggywinkle, Jemima Puddleduck, Tom Kitten, Pigling Bland . . .'

Laura remembered their exchange about Dr Foster who went to Gloucester.

'The light blinded me. A booming voice: "What the fook do you think you're doing on my floor? Rose, to your room now. I'll talk to you in the morning."

'"For god's sake, Dad," said Rose. She did not appear to be discomposed, but she got up obediently. She stood in front of her father for several seconds, forcing him to see her full nakedness. Then she picked up her sweater, her dress and her shoes, tucked them under her arm and marched out of the room. "Get out of my hotel, you little shit."

'I was struggling to make myself decent. Craven, disgusted with myself, I couldn't speak. The proprietor said nothing else, just glared. He had an impressive beard. Like a headmaster, he waited at the foot of the stairs as I stuffed my things into my bag, came back down and handed over the key. "How much? The bill?" "Forget it. Out. Now." The door was locked behind me, the lights snapped off. I did not stop to think. I walked to Town End, to Rydal, to Ambleside. I was at Windermere in time for an early morning train.'

13

The monologue came to an end.

Laura had been bored at first, then rather excited. She had guessed how the story would end. She could see the pattern now. The trouble was, he had again spent so much time on the detail that there were only a few minutes left in which to tease out the essence.

William pulled himself up, sat on the edge of the couch and said to Laura, 'I'd taken my paintbox with me, in case I felt like trying a watercolour of the lake. I was in such a hurry to pack that I left it behind. I don't think I ever bought another one.'

He paused. Then he said, 'I didn't like the way my animal instincts had ruled me. I was afraid I might have caught something. I vowed not to drink again. The article on the literary associations of the Lake District was never written. The only compensation was that I'd got away without paying the hotel bill.'

She smiled at him and was about to pick up on what she took to be the key detail, his remark that the La Touche girl must have regarded Ruskin as a father-figure. What this meant was that he was obsessed with daughter-figures. But he spoke before she could. In the other voice.

In trying to renew old recollections, we cannot as it were unfold the whole web of our existence; we must pick out the single threads.

The tone switched back: 'But then lay the strands together, side by side, and a pattern emerges. Mine is always the same: interruption, unfulfilment. My childhood was broken by the Atlantic crossing. When we set off, I was not the youngest. I think I felt *complete* in the knowledge that one sister came before me and the other came after. I wanted there to be a day when I would be to the baby what Peggy was to me. Then I would still have a sister even as Peggy had grown and left me.'

Laura was affected by this. It sounded real. Maybe the teasing out would not be necessary: he had grasped the kernel for himself.

'Can I really have been shaped by what happened when I was only three?' asked William.

'It has been said,' Laura replied, 'that no one ever changes their character from the time they're two years old – or even from the time they're two hours old.'

She paused for a moment. She saw the paradigm. She tried to think of herself as a replacement for Peggy. It was all a family matter: Fenella, Rose, perhaps even Sally and Sarah, were merely the presenting problem.

Confident that she could make progress by imagining herself as his sister, Laura willed William to imagine the same: 'Suppose I were Peggy and suppose you were close to her again.' She gave him a minute to adjust to the roles.

Then she said, 'Tell me the thing that has affected you most in the time we've been apart.'

She waited. He spoke in the distant voice.

I have never seen death but once, and that was in an infant. It is years ago. The look was calm and placid, and the face was fair and firm. It was as if a wax image had been laid out in the coffin, and strewed with flowers. It was not like death, but more like an image of life. No breath moved the lips, no pulse stirred, no sight or sound would enter those eyes or ears more. While I looked at it, I saw no pain was there; it seemed to smile at the short pang of life which was over: but I could not bear the coffin lid to be closed – it almost stifled me. And still as the nettles wave in a corner of the churchyard over the little grave, the breeze helps to refresh me. It eases the tightness in my chest.

'It wasn't just your baby sister, was it? You lost a child of your own.'

Tears had swollen William's eyes as the words describing the dead baby came from his lips. Now he was sobbing noisily, uncontrollably.

For Laura, this was always the best and the worst moment. The best, because it was the catharsis: she had broken through and reached what was real, the raw emotion. The worst, because she could not allow herself to hold the crying adult. At this time, professional restraint became almost unbearable. Sometimes she thought that the only way she could live with such scenes in her work, week after week, year after year, would be if she had a child of her own whom she could hold and whisper to and comfort.

It was past ten thirty. There was no time, save to let him cry himself out. She gave him tissues instead of instructions. She was fairly sure that the treatment would be over by Friday, or Monday at the latest.

14

It had been a matter of pride to Laura that she should sort it out for herself. She reckoned that she had nearly done so, but she needed confirmation. So on the Thursday evening she phoned Amanda. There was no answer; she left a message on the machine.

'Mand, it's me. Can you do something for me? Which author was it who wrote an essay about a prizefight? Can you tell me anything about his life? Call us back if it's not too late. Love you.'

She went to bed at eleven and read a magazine for half an hour. Just after she had put the light out, the phone rang. It was a slightly drunk Amanda. She had a vague recollection that it was someone in the Romantic period. 'But Romanticism's not my bag,' she went on. 'How urgent is this? I'll check it out with the old boys at work tomorrow.'

Laura was disappointed, but since she was not going to get an answer before the next morning's hour with William, she said that it wasn't especially important, but that she'd very much appreciate it if in their phone call on Sunday Amanda could give her some information about the writer.

She slept badly.

This is what she read on Friday morning.

«« »»

Giving up the day job had been a calculated risk. After the Grasmere business, I was careful to ration the remainder of the money from the Paris articles so that it would last me three months. I lived as simply as I could, but the money was running out and there had been no further commissions. I survived on chicken soup from a tin, making it bearable by adding almonds and raisins. I started drinking coffee instead of tea, since it did more to allay my hunger. For two weeks I lived on almost nothing but the coffee.

I was on the point of resigning myself to a return to menial work, at least part time, when I received a lucky break. I had sent samples of my work to every paper and magazine I could think of, mostly without acknowledgement. One editor had replied encouragingly – 'I like your style. Nothing doing at the moment, but I'll try to push something your way when possible.' That had been two months ago. Now there was a message from him offering me a theatre review.

The piece was a success. I had tipped the hitherto unknown male lead for future stardom and in so doing brought myself into the limelight. As my brother had found in the world of portrait painting, freelance journalism depended on a snowball effect. I found myself a regular berth with a London weekly, doing short reviews of productions 'beyond the West End'.

I grew to love the theatre and to be fascinated by the player's art. I was envious of the actors' ability to *become another*, to be *beside themselves*. I regarded them as the only honest hypocrites, their life as a voluntary dream, a studied madness. I saw myself at second-hand in them: they showed me all that I was, all that I wished to be, and all that I dreaded to be. The stage was like life with the dull part left out. Half-unconsciously, I copied the mannerisms of my favourite performers.

I turned my pen to any subject on which I could get a commission. In lucky periods I was paid to write about what I loved. A friend of a friend worked on a glossy magazine which derived its income from advertisements for fine country properties – I found myself visiting stately homes and reporting on their picture galleries.

The collection at Stourhead is a disappointment, amply made up for by Stourton, the village where the house stands. You descend by a sharp-winding declivity, almost like going underground, between high hedges of laurel trees, and with an expanse of woods and water spread beneath. The inn is like a modernized guardhouse; the village church stands on a lawn without any enclosure; a row of cottages facing it, with their whitewashed walls and flaunting honey-suckles, are neatness itself. Everything has an air of elegance, and yet tells a tale of other times.

It was my first visit to Wiltshire and I fell instantly in love with the county.

I wanted to give a political twist to my articles on the art collections of the stately homes of England.

One sometimes visits an old family-seat, with its moss-grown paling and landscaped park, and fantasizes about spending one's life there in seclusion and content beneath the ancestral oaks, instead of gaining a precarious, irksome and despised livelihood by indulging romantic sentiments and writing disjointed descriptions of them, but the thought has scarcely risen to the lips when we learn that the owner of the blissful domain is a thoroughbred foxhunter, an hereditary peer, a xenophobic Tory – and the dream is shattered.

But I knew that this would not befit the magazine that was paying me, so I did no more than wonder aloud whether certain paintings hung in the private rooms received the appreciation they deserved.

I gained a reputation for being able to hit the house style of each publication for which I wrote, whilst still retaining a voice that was distinctively my own. I was once described as a chameleon in a snide little paragraph in the diary of the London evening newspaper. How could a man, asked my anonymous antagonist, extol the beauties of English villages and 'flaunting honeysuckle' one week, then write like a 'loony leftie' the next?

The Thatcher years. Everybody had an opinion about her. My father despaired. Something I wrote about a new political play – a bitter satire on the quelling of the miners' strike – had brought me to the attention of the newly appointed editor of a radical monthly magazine which was rapidly increasing its circulation by broadening the range of its contributors and the kind of material it covered, aiming to appeal to a new audience of socially concerned young people who had no time for the decaying Labour Party of smoky committee rooms and trade union cabals. I made several contributions which were political in the indirect sense I favoured. They were not about government bills or the adequacy of the leader of the Opposition; they were not about this or that new twist of events, not about what led the news on any one evening. Rather, they were concerned with the debilitation of everyday life, the loss of old communal values, the distance between the politicians and the people, the crumbling infrastructure of society.

My constant theme was that government should be not *of* the people but *for* the people. Politicians had forgotten who the people were – *that they were millions of individuals with thoughts stirring in their minds, with blood circulating in their veins, with wants and appetites and passions and anxious cares and affections for others and a respect for themselves and a desire for happiness and a right to freedom and a will to be free.*

I achieved a certain notoriety with a piece on the return of beggars to the streets of London – not the gnarled cider-drinkers who had always been there, but pale youths, pimpled boys without coats, child-mothers trailing uncomprehending toddlers, shyly holding out an open hand, cowering in anticipation of verbal or even physical abuse. I noted the irony of the prime minister's appeal to 'Victorian values' and of her having set the date of a general election on the anniversary of the birth – or was it the death? – of Charles Dickens. I had the pleasure and the annoyance of hearing my words quoted without acknowledgment on a Labour Party election broadcast.

My article had concluded by suggesting that the only natural course of action available to the people was the removal of the perpetrators of injustice. *When a government, like an old-fashioned building, has become crazy and rotten, stops the way of improvement, and only serves to collect diseases and corruption, and the proprietors refuse to come to any compromise, the community proceed in this as in other cases; they set summarily to work – they pull down the house, they abate the nuisance.*

But publishing where I did, I was preaching to the converted. The people took a different view, Mrs Thatcher was elected for a third term and deep disillusionment fell upon me.

I was no politician and still less of a party man, but I had a hatred of tyranny in all its forms, grand or petty, a contempt for all its tools, for all creatures of power, and this feeling I expressed as often and as strongly as I could. I took my principles from my father: a denial that liberty and slavery were convertible terms, that right and wrong, truth and falsehood, plenty and want, the wellbeing or wretchedness of the people, were matters of indifference. That was all I knew of politics, but on these points I remained incorrigible, however unfashionable and impractical such opinions might be.

In periods when I was not committed to weekly theatre-reviewing, I escaped from London for long weekends. I took to staying at an old inn down in Wiltshire, where I could find a corner to read or write beside a blazing fire. I loved the smell of wood smoke. I would sit for several hours with my eyes fixed upon the fire like a person in a state of deep thought, but thinking nothing.

At such times I felt that I was living in the world as in it, not of it. It was as if no one knew there was such a person as myself and I wished no one to know it. In the corner of the bar I was a silent spectator of the texture of everyday life, not an object of attention or curiosity in it. I would take an anxious interest in what was passing in the world, but not feel the slightest inclination to meddle with it. The mood communicated itself to my writing, and my essays on the times became calm, contemplative, passive, distant. I seemed to smile at the follies of the rich and powerful, but without bitterness. To begin with, my editor on the radical monthly liked the difference in tone from that of the angry fare which filled most of his pages. He said that it gave hope to the reader, served as a reminder that there was a world beyond the dark days of Thatcherism. But in time the commissions became less frequent and then dried up altogether.

In Wiltshire I sometimes wished I had never picked up a pen. Reading was what I loved best, and the advantage of not being a writer was that you could read with delight, without ever having to stop reading in order to start writing. Once you had become a writer, you couldn't prevent yourself being one – you could no longer be *desultory*, could not avoid using your reading, using indeed every experience, as the raw material for writing.

Looking into the fire in which two enormous logs burned slowly off each other, I planned the book I would one day write. After the professor's lecture I had dipped into as many as I could find of the authors he had mentioned, though I don't think I finished any of them. I had given up long ago on reading books through from cover to cover. One of the things that stuck in my mind from the professor's authors was Walter Benjamin's dream of writing a book which consisted entirely of quotations. I liked quotations, aphorisms especially. 'Everyone has one novel in them, but in many cases it doesn't matter whether or not they write it.'

Yes, one day I would write a new kind of book. It would break down the distinction between fact and fiction, creative and critical, primary and secondary. Perhaps it would be a meditation on politics or love or death, both an analysis drawn from my reading and a skewed autobiography drawn from my experience. Something different from all my previous work, the critical reviews and observer's essays. I liked books which mixed up the personal character of the author with general reflections. I thought that the best books were like the best conversations, made up of observations, digressions and anecdotes; a story without application was as tiresome as the kind of long-winded argument which Elder had made his speciality.

But I needed a pattern. I wanted there to be an immediacy, but I didn't want to look too close to home. If only I could find a model in the distant past and make my own present its echo. But how would I ever find time to begin such a book when week by week I had to write to live?

Back to London, to the theatre column, the occasional book review, the frustration of irregular payments. For a time, I supplemented my income by lecturing to evening classes, but I never grew sufficiently confident to do other than read from a prepared script and the time it took to write out each lecture in full made the hourly rate of payment barely worthwhile, much as the idea of lecturing to ordinary working people appealed to me. The delivery of each lecture was time-consumingly rehearsed in front of the mirror.

Had it not been for my wife's small but stable inherited income, I would have found it hard to survive.

How few out of the infinite number of those that marry

and are given in marriage, wed with those they would prefer to all the world: how far the greater proportion are joined together by mere motive of convenience, accident, recommendation of friends, or indeed not infrequently by the very fear of the event, by repugnance and a sort of fatal fascination: yet the tie is for life, not to be shaken off with disgrace or death; a man no longer lives to himself, but is a body (as well as mind) chained to another, in spite of himself.

At last, something more personal. So I am or I was married. But I cannot put a face to her. A voice tells me she was about three years older than me, that when I met her I was still unsure of myself, still hurt by whatever had occurred with Sally, if Sally was the name of my student love. Little else: so few images of my married life. I see myself playing with a cat. I see us laughing together, sharing jokes. Her tongue was sometimes sharp, but her sense of humour always quick. I think she was a good companion. Did I meet her through Charles and Mary, brother and sister, best of companions? We were perhaps like brother and sister. I cannot see her face, but I think I see us sitting by the fireside or sitting down to dinner together – boiled ham with mustard, and potatoes mashed together with parsnips. I never loved her so well as then.

'You please my fancy more then than when I think of you in – no, you would never forgive me if I were to finish the sentence.' Am I imagining it, or did I write that to her in a letter when I was down in Wiltshire, working alone?

I proposed to her while she was putting on the kettle. She knew my preference for Souchong.

But also the memory of hearing a dog bark after we had

made love, then birdsong. It could not have been a marriage wholly without passion.

She never grew her hair for me.

I think we might have had a son. Or was it just that I wanted a son, a young William of my own?

I see myself writing him a letter of fatherly advice as he goes off to boarding school for the first time.

If you think that you do not like school, remember that it is more likely that what you do not like is being away from home; don't be prejudiced about your schoolfellows before you get to know them; never despise anyone for anything they cannot help, least of all for their poverty, which may manifest itself in dress and manner; show neither contempt for those boys who are less quick than you nor admiration for those who are merely stronger or taller than you; the more airs of childish self-importance you give yourself, you will only expose yourself to be the more thwarted and laughed at (that was my hard discovery at your age). True equality is the only true morality or true wisdom. Remember always that you are but one among others, and then you can hardly mistake your place in society. Do not begin to quarrel with the world too soon: for, bad as it is, it is the best we have to live in – here.

Seven years seemed so young for him to be sent away from home; his body was still so slender, so fragile. But I think my wife felt unable to cope with him alone. Her family had the money to pay the fees. I had forfeited my right to have any say in the matter. Besides, she said, he was only going to be a weekly boarder, it was not as if we were sending him out of London or away for whole terms at a time.

I love him so much that I cannot write about him any more. In my published work I often mention my father but rarely my son. That I have lost him is too much to bear. What can have been so strong that I was compelled to leave the marriage, to leave my child?

No sooner do I ask this question than the veil is torn away.

The image of myself I have been projecting here is that projected on the wall behind the word-conjuring lecturer. The painter, the reader, the writer, the man of culture and politics, the modern *philosophe*. It is a false image.

I am back in the Louvre, copying another painting by the same artist. I remember his name now: Jean-Baptiste Siméon Chardin, French, eighteenth-century, recorder of bourgeois life and still life (same difference). John the Baptist, he announces the news of my identity; Simeon, he says *nunc dimittis* (my father died around the time I parted from my wife; he had had a long and happy life, had done his parcel of good for mankind; Dr Shepherd spoke with uncharacteristic measure at his funeral, pronouncing a verdict of *nunc dimittis* – the time was right, enough had been achieved).

My identity, then? Chardin's painting is of a monkey at an easel. With cocked hat and frock coat, elaborate bow tie, he is every bit the gentleman painter. Embroidered kerchief in his pocket. He sits comfortably, almost cockily, one foot resting on the crosspiece at the base of the easel, his tail curled on the floor. In his left paw, he holds palette and brushes and long rule to steady the hand as he paints a straight line with his right. He is looking at his model: a statue of a naked child.

Le singe peintre – an ape, a copyist, not an original artist. A monkey, traditional symbol of lechery. The semblance of a human being, but the slave of his senses, his desire. I am no belated *philosophe*, I am the painting monkey.

15

'I've remembered my wife's name.' He hesitated, as if expecting Laura to play guessing games.

She submitted to the silence. He remained silent for longer than usual, then said in an abashed voice, 'It's Sarah.'

Laura did not reply.

'I'm sure it is. Sarah is my ex-wife. There we were looking for some mysterious stranger and all along it was my wife.'

'Were we looking for a mysterious stranger?'

'I was.'

'What about Sally then?'

'Well, Sally's just a variant of Sarah, isn't it? Maybe my wife's proper name is Sarah but I always called her Sally.'

'Is that the only possibility?'

He thought for a minute. 'Maybe my student lover. Maybe Sally Shepherd – the first girl whose hand I ever touched. Apart from my sister. Or maybe my wife was Sarah and my daughter who died was Sally.'

'So you had a daughter who died as a baby and a son who is still living?'

Edgily he replied, 'To be honest I don't remember whether the baby was a girl or a boy. I can't bear to think about that face again.'

Laura let this go and asked about his son.

'He's called William, of that I'm certain.'

'You and your wife named your son after yourself and, perhaps, your daughter after her?'

'Is that so very strange?'

'You must be keen to see your boy.'

'Of course I am, but I don't know how soon. That rather depends on the circumstances of the divorce.'

'How much do you remember about the divorce?'

'Not much, except that it was my fault.'

'It's never only one person's fault.'

'I was the one who had the affair.' Then he added quickly, 'But the affair wasn't important. A symptom, not a cause. I don't remember anything about the girl. She's not important.'

Laura slowed him down. 'Are you sure she's not important? You said in your writing that it must have been something pretty major to make you leave your son. Couldn't Sarah be the woman you had the affair with?'

He looked startled. Because the thought genuinely had not occurred to him or because she had hit on the truth?

'I don't think so.' If he had denied the possibility more vigorously, she would not have believed him. But this was not a reply worth pushing against. She wanted to handle him gently that morning. He looked as if he had not slept.

When she asked him how he had been affected by the memory of his marriage and his divorce, and the knowledge that he had a son, he said that he had been left drained. She sympathized and told him to take his time. She said some of the things she always said to patients who had been through the trauma of divorce.

Eventually she felt ready to challenge him a little: 'There

was a lot of self-disgust in the last page or two of your writing.'

'I deserted my son. For a casual affair.'

'Deserted is a strong word. You're very hard on yourself.'

A long silence from William, so Laura continues, 'What do you feel about your wife?'

'Nothing very much. I think the divorce has been finalized.'

'In that case, your rights of access to your son will have been agreed. Do you remember where the divorce was filed?'

'I think it might have been Edinburgh. I think that may be why I came to Scotland. Though I don't know why it was Edinburgh, because I'm sure we lived in London, or moved between London and Wiltshire. But that's the first thing I'm going to do when you discharge me – go to the divorce court in Edinburgh and try to trace some details. Get those surnames and addresses your colleague is so anxious about.'

Laura smiled. 'You think you're ready for a discharge, then?'

'Certainly.'

'What about Sarah, the seven-inch conversation, the details of your accident?'

'Sarah was my wife, the seven-inch conversation was my delirium, the accident was an accident.'

'You seem much surer of yourself today, William. Is there anything else you want to tell me?'

'No, I'm very grateful for all you've done.'

'Let me phrase it another way: is there something else you're not telling me?'

'No.'

She knew he was lying, but did not want to say so.

'I asked one of the nurses to keep an eye on you on Wednesday, because you were very upset when you left my office. She said you spent the whole day writing furiously. You must have written more than those ten pages you left for me this morning. Until those last couple of pages, what you gave me was very detached – rather boring, to be honest. It had nothing to do with what you were feeling, with the very real thing that happened in our meeting.'

'I threw away most of what I wrote on Wednesday. It was senseless rambling. I was too upset. I didn't write anything yesterday morning or afternoon – did your spy tell you that?'

'Before I can discharge you, I must be sure that your accident was not an attempt to take your own life and that there is no possibility that you might attempt to do so again.'

'Do I look like the sort of person who would try to top himself? Did I ever, even when I was still lost?'

She didn't answer.

He insisted: 'Did you for one moment think of me as a potential suicide case?'

'It's *your* wellbeing that's our business, William.'

'I'm very well. I don't need any more of your hard-pressed time, your Health Service resources.'

'I'm not sure you're quite ready to go. You're angry with me and that's a sign there's still a lot of stress, a lot of pain, inside you.'

'Psychobabble,' he said. 'Or do you still think I'm fabricating all this?'

'I don't think you're exactly fabricating, but I do think there's still a lot of confusion between yourself and the things you've read. Maybe that's just because you're a writer?'

'Or because of my photographic memory?'

'That's an interesting thought. What do you mean by it?'

'I was thinking about amnesia and its opposite. What's known about photographic memory?'

'The technical term is hypermnesia. It's not been studied in nearly so much detail as amnesia. For obvious reasons – it's not a disorder which needs treatment. But I do recall a remarkable case history by the great Russian neuro-psychologist, Luria.'

'Luria, Laura? Almost your anagrammatic double.'

She indulged his lame word-play with a smile, then told him a little about the case. Over a period of years Luria worked with a man of prodigious memory, whom in the case history he called Veniamin.

Veniamin's mother was cultivated and his father owned a bookshop; his brothers and sisters were quite talented, but had normal memories. When Luria first met him, he gave him words and letters in sequences thirty, fifty, seventy long. Veniamin instantly repeated them back. It was as if he continued to see them: the photographic memory was eidetic, strongly visual.

'Yes,' said William. 'I don't just remember the words describing the fight, I see them on the typed and cyclostyled page where I first read them. The bottom halves of the *y*s are barely visible and all the *e*s are blurred, the effect of the key striking repeatedly against the typewriter ribbon.'

Laura told him some more about Luria's case history.

When he was two or three years old, Veniamin started to learn prayers in Hebrew; he did not understand them, but he remembered them by visualizing them as cloud formations; he still saw them when he heard certain sounds. The photographic memory apparently depends on a strong synaesthetic capacity.

'Yes,' said William again. 'The smell of cardboard or stale alcohol brings back the books I read when I worked in the off-licence.' Then he asked, 'So what would happen if someone afflicted with hypermnesia were blessed with amnesia?'

'You mean if someone blessed with hypermnesia were afflicted with amnesia?'

'I meant what I said.'

Laura looked at him and understood.

'I'm not aware that a case has ever been recorded. But you might be interested to know that Veniamin did find it a terrible affliction to remember everything. His problem was that he had to make himself a better forgetter. He had to teach himself to block things out. In the end, he discovered that the best approach was to *write down* what he wanted to forget. Once something was written, it was forgotten. That way he freed himself to take in new experiences.'

They both understood now. Laura saw that she had to let him go. He would write for the rest of the day and through the weekend. By Monday, the treatment would be complete. Her talking cure had helped, but the true cure had been the writing.

'You remember everything now, William. Go and write it down, so that you can then forget it again. Spend the weekend writing. Come and see me on Monday morning and tell me as much or as little as you like. Then I'll give you your discharge papers and we can say goodbye.'

She paused before adding, 'And it must be goodbye for good. If you do decide on follow-up psychotherapy – which I strongly recommend – then it must be with someone else.'

The hour was not over, but the time for conversation had passed. She knew that what he needed was his pen and paper. She stood up and showed him to the door, where she shook his hand. It was their first touch.

16

Sunday evening. The phone rings. She's expecting Amanda. The information about the writer. The completion of the jigsaw.

It's the hospital. Informing her that the patient 'William' has not been seen since the middle of the day. Can she come in?

She drives straight over. She is not surprised, just mildly annoyed. A little disappointed in him for not waiting till the next day, when he would have been given an official discharge.

The usual procedure is followed. The police are informed. She has no address or likely destination to give them. She tells them that the patient is neither psychotic nor suicidal, certainly no danger to the public.

All that he has left behind is his writing pad.

She takes it to her office. She intends only to flick through it. She can look at it properly back home over a large brandy, after speaking to Amanda.

But once she begins, she is unable to break away. She's missing William. She wants to be Sarah. She despises herself.

This is what she reads.

II

Sarah

1

I had been living apart from my wife for the previous two years.

Deliberately or not, I was killing the marriage by starving it of its necessary lifeblood, that total intuitive knowledge of the other which comes only from daily companionship. But I often wondered if it was an illusion, this assumption of mine that one could read the soul of another.

My friend Mary, who had introduced me to Ms Stoddart and who would be her sole bridesmaid, told me shortly after my engagement that my fiancée's grand failing was secrecy. 'Her brother is the same,' Mary had continued, 'so I would say it is a family failing – by secrecy, I mean that they haven't got the habit of telling each other everything that happens at the moment it happens.' Seeing my frown, she added, 'But everybody has *one* fault and there are far worse than this. It won't get in the way of your happiness.' And she hugged me. I did not dwell on what she had said, for I knew that Charles and Mary's standards of openness and their habit of telling each other everything that happens at the moment it happens were quite exceptional.

Perhaps I should have been made to hesitate. For me, love meant being constantly inside the other's mind, it meant a perpetual telepathy, the finishing of each other's sentences, the occurrence of the same thought at the same moment. It meant waking up and whispering one's dreams, discovering you had both dreamed the same thing at the same moment. For a few, quick bright months when I had been an art student, this was how it had seemed to be with Sally, the first and only love of my life. But I had been so scarred by the night when Sally had told me she'd slept with a classmate whom I had regarded as a friend that when I proposed marriage to the witty and (by my standards) wealthy Stoddart girl it seemed to me safe and sane that when we looked at each other our eyes did not burn through to the other's soul as I believed my eyes and Sally's had done.

Once, about six months into the marriage, I met Sally in the street. We exchanged a few fraught words. I could not get the three words of cliché out of my head: my old flame.

A few nights later I dreamed of her. I tried to tell my wife about this, to explain about the relationship and my subsequent near-breakdown, the salvation of my sanity through work and work and work, my vow never to let the madness of passion afflict me again, my sense of security in the light of the lower but steadier flame which burned between us. But she did not want to know, she said that some things should be kept secret. Our son was born a year after this and there was no more room for passion or reflection on the lack of it.

Then the baby died. Our pain became anger towards each other. Another boy was born. We named him William – William the Second, we sometimes called him. To others, the nickname was the result of the son being named after the father; for us, it was a way of remembering our first son.

As the boy grew, our doting on him increased in proportion with our distance from each other.

I had spent more and more time down in Wiltshire, found it more and more difficult to work in the company of my wife and son. I had tried moving out for a short period and it gradually became clear that I would not move back in, though I took my boy to the park or the zoo most weekends. There was no incentive to divorce.

I liked the freedom of living in bedsits, or 'studio apartments' as the letting agencies insisted on calling them. I liked the bareness of rented rooms, their anonymity broken only by the books I had with me (I could change them for others when I went home at the weekends) and the mounted engravings and curled postcards I placed on mantelpiece, table or windowsill. And I liked the ease with which I could move out and move on when the fancy took me to live in a different part of London. But after two years I decided I wanted something different: an old-fashioned lodging house, where I wouldn't have to bother with any domestic chores.

It had taken considerable effort to find one. It seemed that there wasn't the demand any more. Students and secretaries wanted more independence; business trainees could afford better.

The landlady, visibly overweight in her slacks, but confident in the memory of how she had always been an object of male regard, showed me to my new room. She explained that she usually had three or four 'gentlemen' in her care. They sometimes stayed for more than two years. My room was that little bit cheaper because it was slightly smaller than the others, but she always included daily breakfast in the price. The custom was that breakfast would be brought to me in my room at a regular time, which I could specify, each morning.

The price was high for the size of room, but the difficulty it had taken to find anything comparable, together with the prospect of breakfast, clinched my acceptance. The building was located in a conveniently central part of London. I had grown tired of long tube journeys after first nights; here, I could walk back from the theatres, composing my review in my head. A proper breakfast would be just the thing: when I was writing, I liked to eat at the beginning of the day, then consume nothing save frequent mugs of tea until I had completed my ration of ten pages. I would then eat in the early evening before going to the theatre or the cinema or settling down to a book.

In bedsit land I had got into the habit of making myself a large bowl of porridge to accompany the two mugs of tea with which I always started the day. If 'Mrs W.', as she'd told me her 'gentlemen' always called her, brought me a substantial breakfast, I would need nothing else for the rest of the day save my box of Souchong teabags and my electric kettle. I established the size of breakfast. Begrudgingly, Mrs W. accepted my condition that the hard edges should be pared off my buttered toast, since I found them hurtful to my gums.

I usually read late into the night to the quiet accompaniment of the BBC World Service on my little radio, and I was not good at getting up in the mornings, so I staked a claim for half past nine as my regular breakfast hour. Mrs W. seemed to have mixed feelings about this. She was pleased that it meant breakfasts would be staggered – her other gentlemen would be well out of the way by that time (she fixed me with a look that asked sceptically what kind of work it was I did that allowed me to laze around till half nine in the morning). But she also muttered something about God only knowing what time Sarah would get down to anything useful about the house if she wasn't through with breakfast and its consequences till nearly eleven o'clock. I assumed that Sarah must have been a woman brought in to help with the washing up and housework.

I took no interest in the other lodgers, although I soon became conscious of a loud and obviously drunken Welsh voice on the stairs late at night. The first few mornings Mrs W. brought the breakfast herself – 'I always like to make sure that my new gentleman is settling in, can I draw the curtains for you? No? Well, please yourself. I'd be most obliged if you could leave the tray outside the door when you've finished.'

On the Saturday, there was a much quieter tap at the door. Fixing my half-open eye on the spot where Mrs W.'s head always appeared, I was baffled for a moment because I saw no one. Then I looked down several inches and caught the mildly apprehensive eye of a girl of about thirteen. 'Good morning, sir, here's your breakfast.' She said that she was Lizzy, the youngest daughter, and that she earned some extra pocket money by helping at weekends and in the school holidays. She was inquisitive about my work; I tried to explain what a freelance writer does. She had a delicate, elfin face and I realized for the first time that the mother would have been very attractive in her youth.

I declined Sunday breakfast, preferring to sleep in until lunchtime. Since leaving home, I seemed to need much more sleep – or I could allow myself much more, William the Second not being there to demand attention.

On the Monday I awoke before nine. It was the first sunny day since I had moved in, and I was pleased to discover that my room faced east. A shaft of August sunlight had worked its way in through the crack in the curtains and fallen across my bed. I lay looking at the ceiling, planning my week's work.

The tread outside the door was lighter than that of Mrs W. Since it was summertime, it could have been Lizzy earning holiday money. But the knock sounded more purposeful and confident than the girl's, though quieter than the mother's.

Love at first sight is only realizing an imagination that has always haunted us – our dream is out at last.

For a moment I thought I was still asleep and dreaming. Her back, which I saw first, was straight as a wand. Her long dark hair tumbled in waves; her light-complexioned face was perfectly proportioned with high cheekbones and strong profile. I was instantly reminded of a painting, but could not remember the artist or the gallery where I had seen it. My first thought was: if I were still a painter I would always paint her, she would be my model for everything I do from this day till the day I put down my brush for the last time. My second thought was: this is the face I want to wake beside every day for the rest of my life.

'Classical' was the word that kept reverberating in my head; classical beauty, something you read about in aesthetic theory, something you see in a painting or statue, but what is classical beauty doing in a shabby London lodging house? Surely she would only have to walk down the street for a photographer or designer to say, 'Come with me and I will give you a fabulous future in modelling.' 'Model' was the other word that echoed: she could have been a model, I wanted her to be my model, she was a model of classical beauty, she was in some indefinable sense a model not a human being. There was a poise about her, a feline quality to her movement across the room, that set her apart. Ordinary people, misshapen, ill at ease in their bodies, did not move like this. Her face was pale, cold even, in the morning sunlight: a model, not of wax but of marble.

My love for Shakespeare had grown through my years of theatre reviewing. I felt closest to the late plays, and it was them that this young woman instantly brought to mind. She was Marina, Perdita, Miranda; she was the embodiment of youth, hope, fresh life. She was the thou that rebegot the him that did her beget. She was the spring. My imagination was working at a furious pace. It had already put her on stage with flowers in her hair; I was young again myself, was holding her two hands in my outstretched hands and spinning her, swinging her around and around and around and saying as she came to a halt, breathing slightly more quickly but perfectly balanced, perfectly poised, her smile the smile of nature with not the slightest shadow of art or artifice,

> When you do dance, I wish you
> A wave o' th' sea, that you might ever do
> Nothing but that; move still, still so,
> And own no other function. Each your doing,

So singular in each particular,
Crowns what you are doing in the present deeds,
That all your acts are queens.

But in the same instant I thought of a different moment in the same play, my favourite moment in the whole of Shakespeare. She was not Perdita but Hermione, she was the statue which came to life in the final scene. Warm life, as now it coldly stands: her face that seemed cold with the slickness of marble was slowly colouring, I was holding her and sobbing, 'O, she's warm, she's warm, if this be magic, then let it be an art as lawful as weeping.' Hot tears were pricking my eyes: I had waited so, so long for this moment. How many years had it been since Sally was lost to me? Fourteen? Sixteen?

I had lectured on *The Winter's Tale* in one of my evening classes, and I remembered my words about this moment, though I did not stop to reflect on what might be learnt from them.

'Shakespeare's model here is the most famous classical myth of artistic creation: Pygmalion and his ivory image of a beautiful girl. Pygmalion carves a statue so realistic that it seems to be of nature not art, so beautiful that he falls in love with it. He desperately wants to believe it is real and there are moments when the perfection of the art is such that the statue does seem to be struggling into life. Then Venus, the goddess of love, takes pity on the artist, his wish is fulfilled and a kiss brings the statue to softness, warmth and colour. The artist is allowed to make love to his own creation. If you want something badly enough and you believe in it hard enough, you will eventually get it.

When Hermione descends and embraces Leontes, she *is* warm.'

'Shall I draw the curtain?'

'No, not these twenty years.'

'I beg your pardon, sir?'

I hesitated for a moment, unable to believe that I could have thought so much in the few seconds during which she had bent to pick up the tray which she must have placed on the landing floor as she opened the door, stood for an instant with her back to the room, the doorway framing her like the proscenium arch of a stage, turned so that I saw her face for the first time (she had avoided eye contact, and I wondered if this had been deliberate, an effect of shyness), taken a few steps across the room, put down the tray, and spoken.

Collecting myself: 'No, yes, why not halfway, so that the sun can come in some more but not altogether dazzle me.' The sentence of an embarrassed schoolboy unused to the company of girls, not of a published writer, I thought to myself wryly.

For a second time she stood framed, this time by the window. Back-lit by the sun, there was a sheen to her hair, a pinprick of colour blushing her face. Did she stand in that pose a second longer than was natural or was my racing pulse measuring time at a different speed from that at which it was actually passing?

'Will there be anything else this morning, sir?'

Another pause. How to keep her here, keep her talking. Flailing madly for an opening, but nothing. Nothing but her face, her straight figure. 'No, nothing, I don't think so.' She hesitated for another moment, as if to give me a second chance. Surely there was something I could ask her. Still nothing, and she was gone, gliding out of the room like an apparition in a play. She had paused for a moment in the doorway and turned her head back towards me, framed for the third time.

As soon as she was gone, I realized that I could have asked her name and struck up a conversation as I had done with Lizzy (though in fact it had been Lizzy who had initiated the dialogue). I lay for a full further half hour before going over to the table. The toast was by then like leather, the egg inedible, the cereal soggy and the tea cold. There was no taste to the food.

I had been trying to fix the face and the figure in my mind, but maddeningly it kept slipping away. Why was she so damned elusive: I was an artist, I had a good eye. I had become adept at conjuring on to the page the image of an actress in full flow, so why could I not hold her in the eye of my mind? I had to see her again, to fix the image.

Mrs W. had initially been uneasy about my habit of working in my room for much of the day. When would she be able to get in to clean and tidy and make the bed? – making the bed daily and changing the sheets weekly was one of the little services that her gentlemen appreciated, one of their incentives not to move on too soon. I had appeased her by saying that I would go out for a walk every afternoon at two o'clock, whatever the weather. The early afternoon was the low point of my day. The walks cleared my head – the room was small – and I found that, provided I did not linger in the little nearby square too long, provided I was climbing the stairs again no later than five past three, I would be able to set to work with renewed vigour, fortified by another mug of tea. That first week, my best writing had been produced between the hours of three and five, with the bed neatly made.

It now occurred to me that since I was always out at the time, I could not be sure that the room was done by Mrs W. herself. Then I remembered her muttered remark about Sarah. This girl must be Sarah, employed to clean and clear up. There was an excellent chance that it was she who came into my room each day at two o'clock. I was sensitive to smell and I now fancied that on the first occasion when I had returned at three, there had been a sweetish scent in the air of the room, very different from the faintly sweaty aura which Mrs W. carried in each morning with the breakfast tray.

I convinced myself that the room now had its afternoon smell, not its morning one, and that this was proof that it was Sarah who made my bed each day. If I stayed in, I would see her again in less than four hours. It would be hard to explain why I had decided not to go out for my turn in the fresh air on the first fine day since my arrival. But I could claim that I was up against a deadline.

I took a little longer than usual in the bathroom. I wrote nothing all morning. There were often mornings when I got no further than an opening paragraph – beginning was always the hardest thing for me – but I no longer worried about this, for I knew that the late afternoons would generally provide ample compensation, my fingers hammering on the typewriter keys (I had started my career as a writer on a typewriter and refused to move to a word processor, however vigorously my editors extolled their virtues or spoke of the ease of revision – I always replied that I liked my typewriter precisely because revision was hard work, because if you changed one sentence you had to re-type the whole page and that encouraged you to improve other sentences). To write not a single word was, however, exceptional.

At ten past two, there was a knock on the door. My throat went dry: I knew from its lightness that it was Sarah. Trying to prevent my voice from quavering, I called out, 'Yes.' Mrs W. walked in.

'I thought I hadn't heard you going out at two, so I gave a little tap instead of barging in like normal. What should I do? Are you going on out later? You really ought to, it's a lovely day. Fancy you staying in on the first sunny afternoon we've had for goodness' knows how long. Or I could make the room up around you. It wouldn't do no harm to leave the hoovering till tomorrow.'

I was coming slowly down, my heart returning to its regular beat. Embarrassed, annoyed with myself for breaking my routine, I said, 'I was just on my way out – I was finishing something, but I'll go now.'

She told me not to hurry for her sake, not to mind her. I left immediately, with a distracted 'No, no, no'. She clucked and shook her head. Temperamental types, these writers, by all accounts. Still, he was quiet enough – never came in drunk like Griffiths. And having a writer in the house was something a little bit different, something to talk about. 'Perhaps he'll put you all in his novel,' her son had said when he was over for his usual Wednesday evening meal.

'He's a critic, not a novelist,' Lizzy had replied in a proprietorial voice.

'What's the difference?' asked Mr W., looking up from his paper.

'A critic is someone who's failed as a writer himself, so he spends his time criticizing other writers,' said his son smugly.

'He's a dramatic critic,' retorted Lizzy, still defensively.

'You'll be scrounging free tickets off him next,' her brother came back at her, and then the subject was changed.

Imagining such a conversation in order to take my mind off Sarah, I sat in the square, confused by the strength of my feelings. When had my blood last surged as it had that morning? Many times on seeing a fine prospect as I walked in the country, on looking at a painting or reading a line of poetry. Occasionally in the theatre or the cinema. But never with a person, in the flesh, and never so intensely as this. Unless, perhaps, with Sally, but of my time with her I had no recollection. Certainly never in my marriage. Friendship, courtship, consummation, fatherhood: all had brought warmth and contentment. When I held my child for the first time, tears streamed down my face. But they were warm tears, not hot. This heat in the blood, this burning of the palate, was new. Its uncontrollability scared me.

The room was tidy when I returned. The rest of the day a blank. The night sleepless. In the darkness, the image of Sarah became clearer – or was I painting it for myself? Tall, her back straight as a wand, her dark hair long, curled gently into waves as it dropped and rocked. The face still elusive. My body strained. I enjoyed the sensation, the absence of the relief which would have made me drowsy. I did not want to sleep. Perversely, I wanted to stretch out the time until she came to me in the morning.

As on nights of old when I had read philosophy or talked with Elder through the small hours, I passed a point after which I was no longer tired. I had renewed energy, was thinking with absolute clarity. I had the morning's conversation fully prepared.

When she came in, I was immediately the gawky schoolboy once more. The prepared conversation had gone: the lines of a nervous actor who has been word-perfect in the dress but dries on press night. She met my eye for the first time. The black centre, the whiteness around. 'It's sunny again.'

'Yes, about time we had a run of good days.'

'You spend a lot of time in your room, you ought to get out in the sun more.'

'So you're a creature of the sun, are you . . .' – I paused, because I was squirming inside at how corny I must have sounded, but she must have imagined I was searching for her name.

'Sarah.'

Now that I had seen her face properly, I realized that she was no hired maid, she must be another of Mrs W.'s daughters. Lizzy was going to be very pretty too.

'Are you a big family? I've only met Lizzy till now.'

'My older sister's married, and Caj, my brother, he's left home, though he comes round quite often. It's just Lizzy and me otherwise.'

'She's a nice kid.'

'I better get on, unless there's anything else. Leave the tray outside, so I don't disturb you later.'

'I don't mind being disturbed by you – I mean, it's nice

to see another face when you're cooped up alone writing all day.'

'Mum said you were a writer – though anyone'd've guessed from all those books and papers.'

She had gone, like a sylph, before I had time to start telling her about my writing.

From then on, Sarah brought up the tray almost every morning and I always detained her in conversation for as long as I could. We began with the weather; she told me what she had done the previous evening (what had been on television, what so-and-so had said at the pub) and what she had to do that day (hoover the stairs, walk Lizzy home from school); I told her about my work. She appeared to be impressed when I told her one day that I was writing about a play I had seen the previous night, and then two days later showed her a printed column in the newspaper with my name at the head of it. I was then mildly taken aback when she added, 'I knew you wrote those review things because I saw one of them on your desk when I was tidying up the first week you were here.'

Some mornings I talked about world affairs, remarking on a report I had heard on the World Service during the previous night; she complained about her mother and described a lovely skirt she'd seen in Top Shop. She seemed willing to linger, though I suspected that this was more as an excuse for not getting down to the washing-up and housework than out of genuine interest in my company.

One morning, to my intense disappointment, Mrs W. bustled in. Sarah had been sent out on some errand. 'I hope that girl's not distracting you from your work with her chatter every morning.' I assured her that I always gave the girl her marching orders – my ear was now tuned to my landlady's chosen idioms – as soon as I was ready to start work. In fact it was always Sarah who decided when she would slip out of the room – usually just as the conversation was beginning to take a more personal turn, to go beyond matters of what we had done towards questions of who we were. On one occasion, though, she had asked about the photograph on my desk, and I had told her about William the Second.

I liked young Lizzy, but approached the end of each week with gloom. For two mornings I would be deprived of my fix of Sarah. On weekdays I found that I was always awake before nine thirty, mentally preparing myself for my precious five or ten minutes. At weekends, the alarm of my internal clock knew that it did not need to sound.

2

It was September now, my fourth Saturday in the lodging house. I had slept deeply for the first time in the nineteen nights since Sarah had backed into my room. I was dreaming of her. In my dream I was for the first time close enough to her to see that her eyes were brown. She was sitting on the end of the bed, holding something that I had written and looking at me with admiration.

I opened my eyes.

She did not blush.

'Wakey-wakey – there was no reply when I knocked, so I came in to put the tray on the table for you. I was just looking at the writing that was on the desk. I hope you don't mind. What's it about?'

I must have been still half asleep, because what I said next I would never have said if I had been fully conscious of what I was saying.

'Don't you find it hard being so beautiful?'

Still she did not blush, but she looked away from me for a moment, half-closing her wide brown eyes.

'Sometimes I get tired of people trying to possess me,' she said. 'Imagining they can just touch me when they want to – men in bus queues and that.'

A pause.

'Mum and Dad have taken Lizzy out for the day. They're meeting my sister and her husband.'

How was I to read this? An explanation of the fact that she, rather than her little sister, had brought the tray? The waking answer. Or an invitation? The dream.

'Sarah, will you get into bed with me?'

I often thought back on this moment, because it seemed to me that it was the only time I ever surprised her. She was so attractive that she must have had frequent propositions, but I guessed that she was used to boys working up to things gradually – a date, a kiss, a first tentative feel, ground rules of progression. And usually a gesture would have come first. They would have reached out and pulled her towards them (I hate the thought of anyone else touching her), she would have accepted or resisted. They wouldn't have simply made the request verbally, matter-of-factly, out of the blue. I wouldn't have done so if I had been aware of what I was doing.

A longish pause. Then, with a slight whine of reproach, 'But you're married.'

Hurrying to find an answer. 'You know we're living apart. And what goes on within any marriage is a mystery.'

Another pause, of briefer duration. 'I don't have sex.'

I was not sure exactly what this meant.

'I just want to hold you.'

Then with almost too much alacrity: 'All right, but just a cuddle.'

And she was in the single bed beside me, though she immediately turned her back.

I was wide awake now. Life stood in the level of my dream.

Neither of us spoke. I buried my face in her hair, adoring

its soft texture. I placed a tentative arm around her waist, marvelling at its slenderness and firmness. She neither tensed nor relaxed, neither resisted nor encouraged, neither pulled away nor pressed in. Neither of us spoke.

I began to stroke her hair. I moved my other hand up her bare arm. She was wearing a loose light-green T-shirt of brushed cotton. I moved my hand slowly; her arm was long. The flesh goose-pimpled, the hairs stood up, and I thought I detected a slight softening of her breathing. I rubbed her shoulder through the cotton, then held it tightly. I could not help noticing that I could not feel a strap.

I broke the silence. 'Sarah.'

She did not reply.

I said 'Sarah' twice more, very quietly.

She did not reply.

I asked her if she had a second name.

'Jane,' she said, in a voice that sounded resentful.

I whispered 'Sarah Jane', three, four, five times, very slowly. She seemed to relax a tiny amount. I moved my right hand down, still stroking her hair with my left. I ran my fingers over hers. Her hand was folded, defensively. I stroked the back of it. The skin was very soft. Again, she seemed to relax a little. I locked my fingers into hers. She made no attempt to withdraw them, nor did she squeeze my hand in return when I pressed harder. We lay in silence for what seemed to me like a glorious eternity, but what was in all probability no more than about two minutes. I somehow sensed that her eyes were open, unblinking, staring almost vacantly into the middle distance of the room.

I murmured 'Sarah' again, untwined my hand and cupped it over her right breast. As I had thought, she was wearing nothing beneath the T-shirt.

I peised the breast, which was firm and soft and warm all at once. I told myself that it was meant for me. To hold it was to have come home, a place I had never been with my wife. I pressed myself harder against Sarah's back. My erection had to be apparent to her now, but still she neither inched away nor pressed in return.

Time again stood still. To hold this moment for ever, hold this breast for ever. A word would have broken the spell.

I moved my right hand down, brushing it against the outer side of her thigh. She had a model's legs and this morning, as on most mornings, their contours were easily traceable through her black leggings. She was wearing a short black skirt.

I seemed to know that if I did not speak – save to whisper her name – the spell would not break, the next step could be taken. I worked my hand under the T-shirt and upwards on to her breast. The flesh was hot, but without sweat and as smooth as the silk of soft romance.

For the first time, I was struck by the oddity of the situation. A respected writer in his mid-thirties, married but separated; a cool observer of culture and politics, sometime painter, philosopher-*manqué*. In a time-warped London lodging house on a Saturday morning in early September, lying on his side in a single bed, holding the breast of a girl he hardly knew – a girl whose age he did not know (eighteen?) – a girl whose universe revolved around TV and Top Shop – a girl who lay as still as a mannequin and let him do this to her. A girl whom he adored and worshipped and for whom he would gladly have lain down his life. The wretched thing about clichés, he thought, is that they are so damn true.

I must have been moving my fingers over her nipple. She moaned quietly for the first time and turned towards me, pressing her face into my shoulder. Her arms were half around me. Her face was buried, so I could not kiss her.

Convinced that if only I remained silent the dream would continue, I began to nuzzle the back of her neck with my lips, parting strands of hair with my fingers. This caused her to let out some of the tension with which she had been holding herself. For the first time I felt that she was enjoying being in my arms. I kissed the side of her white neck. I worked my way round to just below her chin and suddenly she moaned loudly. Her hands stretched out across my back, her long nails digging slightly into my flesh through my pyjamas. It occurred to me that she was probably not used to men in pyjamas. Her boyfriends probably slept naked or wore nothing but boxer shorts. I had a horrible image of her in the pub telling a girlfriend about my striped pyjamas, giggling at my expense.

But I had found the spot with this part of her neck; now she was pushing against me, welcoming me. She took my hand and put it back under her T-shirt, pressed it against her breast, holding her hand over mine as her nipple hardened again. Her body was now arched into mine, working rhythmically. For the first time I began to feel strain and shame – I must not burst, I must not end it.

I ran my other hand the full length of her leg, sliding my finger over her muscular calf – all those stairs, so many times a day – before curling my hand round her thigh. Again, her hand was on top of mine, moving it into position.

Thinking back, later in the day, I could not remember whether it was with wonder or with shock that I had found my hand between her legs, that I had felt the hard ridge of bone just above, then the soft give of the place itself, that I had sensed her breathing quicken, then slow. Before any of this sunk in, she was gone.

3

As I lay looking at the ceiling, the sounds of London – motorcycles, horns, a distant siren – gradually filtered their way back into the room. I was still throbbing, though of course I wondered if it might all have been a dream. But the sheets of the essay I had been writing the previous night lay on the floor at the bottom of the bed and the now-familiar breakfast tray was on the desk.

Why had she done it? What had been in it for her? She had let me hold her, let me softly repeat her name. I was in love and it was going to be requited. I had found my model and she loved me. What was loveliest of all was that she had been too modest to say anything and that to begin with she had shyly turned her back. The grace of this action was enough to make me weep.

That afternoon I decided to write something new. The book I had vowed I would one day begin. The work that was not critical, the thing into which I would pour my whole being. It would be a meditation on the nature of love.

Leave a lover alone with his thoughts for twelve hours and what happens? I remembered the story about the salt mines of Salzburg.

Where had I read it?

They throw a leafless winter branch into the abandoned workings and when they take it out some months later, it is shimmering with a crystal deposit. A bare branch has become a million diamonds. That is what happens in the mind of the lover: every thought is a crystallization, every circumstance becomes proof of the perfection of the beloved.

I wrote all afternoon, all evening, intensely focused, strangely at ease. The last thing that seemed necessary was to see Sarah again. It was one o'clock in the morning when I stopped. I put on my dressing gown and made for the bathroom. In the dark on the landing, there was a grunt and a thud. I flicked on the light. On the floor, stark naked, reeking of beer, his thick wedge pointing straight up towards me, lay Griffiths, the Welshman whose Saturday-night drinking exploits were a lodging-house legend. 'Jusht going for a pee,' he said, taking three attempts to rise to his feet. I returned to my room and waited for a quarter of an hour before going back to perform my own ablutions.

Lizzy brought in the Sunday breakfast. I asked her if she'd enjoyed her day out. Yes, they had been to the zoo, which was still her favourite thing to do, even though she was twelve now. I said that my son loved the zoo too. We watched the chimps together for hours. For a moment I felt guilty that my love for Sarah had in no time come to mean more to me than my child. Lizzy said: 'Will you excuse me, I've got to do everything for Mum today, since Sarah's out with her *friend*.'

Did *friend* mean boyfriend? But how could she have done what she did yesterday and go out with a boyfriend today? I would not rest till I had challenged her about this. Then I remembered that I had arranged to spend the day with William the Second.

In the park I was irritable, taking out my fear and confusion on my son. No, we couldn't go to McDonald's – we were always going, hamburgers were bad for you, the bright lights and garish colours made Daddy's head ache. The boy was for once glad to be returned to his mother.

I hung around the hall and the stairs for as long as I could, found excuses to leave my room once every half-hour through the evening, desperately hoping to catch Sarah as she came in. The house was quiet.

A restless night, in contrast to the previous one, when, blessed by the holding and the writing, I had slept like a child.

Still no sign on Monday morning – Mrs W. with the tray, in a bad mood, not answering my casual inquiry after Sarah. I couldn't work. Mrs W. at two for the cleaning. In the evening I felt I had to get out of the house.

When she came in on the Tuesday morning, Sarah acted as if nothing had happened.

«« »»

My wrist is tired. I have been holding the pen between my fingers, emptying it in smooth motion across the faintly ruled lines for more than seven hours. I have filled just over twenty pages. So that the ink does not blot, I write only on one side of each leaf. Each page takes approximately twenty minutes. My concentration was broken just once, when an ancillary worker tried to persuade me to go to lunch. I declined – you can get away with skipping the odd meal before the nurses are on to you.

Also just once, I paused of my own volition, sensing a natural break some time between the apparition and the consummation. But what kind of consummation could it be called?

Drained, I forget what it is I have written, though I know it is something important. The threads are still brittle, easily snapped. Then I re-read it and fix the memory. Every detail is still vivid. This was the turning point of my life.

When I cried in Laura's room this morning, it was at first for my baby who died. But then it was for the love that I have made myself kill. My love for Sarah.

A part of me wants to rush and tell Laura that I have found Sarah. It is not quite six o'clock, the time at which I have sometimes seen her leave. I might be able to catch her. Or even tell them it's an emergency and get her home number.

A more sensible part is profoundly embarrassed by what I have read. I am lucky that I have two nights and a day before I see Laura again; by Friday I will be more in control. The slow piecing-together of my childhood, my adolescence and my work-self has not prepared me for this *coup de foudre*. The man about whom I have been writing with such utter absorption seems on re-reading to be a middle-aged fool.

'A distant siren'? And the unforgiveable knowledge: 'My love for Sarah had in no time come to mean more to me than my child.'

I need air. I must walk in the grounds as the sun goes down. The Scottish days are getting shorter now, but the yellowing leaves are beautiful in the late afternoon light.

«« »»

Later. While I was walking I heard the inner voice. I know that Laura is attracted to it and not to me.

The sight of the setting sun does not affect me so much from the beauty of the object itself, from the glory kindled through the glowing skies, the rich broken columns of light, or the dying streaks of day, as that it indistinctly recalls to me numberless thoughts and feelings with which, through many a year and season, I have watched its bright descent. It is because natural objects have been associated with childhood play, with air and exercise, with feelings in solitude when the mind takes the strongest hold on things; with change of place, the pursuit of new scenes, and thoughts of distant friends; it is because they have sur-rounded us in almost all situations, in joy and in sorrow, in pleasure and in pain; because they have been one chief source and nourishment of our feelings, and a part of our being, that we love them as we do ourselves. Nature always wears one face, and speaks the same well-known language, striking on the heart amidst unquiet thoughts and the tumult of the world, like the music of one's native tongue heard in some far-off country.

. «« »»

Friday.

I slept badly on Wednesday night, the night after the day in which my tears and then my pen brought Sarah back. Yesterday morning I could not settle to the task. It was almost as if I was scared of what I would discover next, what new humiliation would follow. An empty day.

Not ready to give my book of love to Laura, I wrote

some other stuff in the evening. More of the usual history of my work, but a little about my wife and my son – enough to give us fifty minutes' conversation without getting too close to Sarah.

This morning's appointment was at nine thirty, as usual. Strange that I see Laura for a morning hour, as I saw Sarah.

I pretended that I had been drained by the discovery of my lost child, my living child, my marriage, my divorce. I think I managed to convince her that Sarah was the name of either my wife or my dead baby. I don't know why, but I didn't want to tell her that the baby was a boy. We agreed that after a final meeting on Monday I would be ready for a formal discharge. She let me go early.

Now I am trying to forget the events of the first month in the lodging house. To concentrate instead on the book about love which I had remembered beginning. Did I complete it? Did I publish it? What had been my thoughts on love? Nothing comes into my head save a few fragmentary aphorisms. As always with the generalities, as opposed to the trivialities which I know are mine, and the day-by-day events which are beginning to ground me, I am unsure whether I did once write these words or whether they are stitched together from my reading. Memories or translations?

Still, to commit them to paper will be a way of making myself write about the past again. Some sound like statements of the moment, others have the coolness of retrospection.

A woman establishes her power by granting favours. The glance is her most powerful weapon.

'Love at first sight' is not so great an absurdity as it is

sometimes imagined to be. We generally make up our minds beforehand as to the sort of person we should like – pensive or smiling, dark or light, with the poet's 'golden tresses' or 'raven locks' – and when we meet with a complete example of the qualities we admire, the bargain is soon struck. We have never before seen anything to come up to our newly discovered goddess, but she is what we have been all our lives looking for. The idol we fall down before and worship is an image familiar to our minds. It has been present to our waking thoughts, it has haunted us in our dreams.

Stepping out of the carriage, Goethe's Werther sees Charlotte for the first time (and falls in love with her), framed by the door of her house (cutting bread and butter for the children): the first thing we love is a scene. For love at first sight requires the very sign of its suddenness (what makes me irresponsible, subject to fatality, swept away, ravished): and of all arrangements of objects, it is the scene which seems to be best for the first time: a curtain parts: what had not yet ever been seen is discovered in its entirety and then devoured by the eyes: what is immediate stands for what is fulfilled: I am initiated: the scene consecrates the object I am going to love. For ever afterwards that first scene will inhabit the lover's memory.

The propensity to dissolve into tears is a disposition proper to the amorous type. He flouts the censure which today forbids adult tears and by which a man attempts to protest his virility. By releasing his tears without constraint, the lover follows the order of the amorous body, which is a body in liquid expansion. The lover obtains the right to cry by rediscovering the infant body. Babies and lovers find peace at the nipple.

The problem for a thinking man is that love is like a fever. It is born and it vanishes without the will playing the smallest part in the matter.

A mark of love's recent birth: all the pleasures and all the pains provoked by all other passions and all other needs instantly stop affecting us.

From the moment he falls in love, even the wisest man no longer sees any object as it really is. The sight of any great beauty, in nature or art, brings back the memory of the beloved with the rapidity of lightning. So it is that a love of the beautiful and love itself give each other life.

Her beauty is nothing other than the sum of all the fulfilments of all the desires which you have successively formed with regard to her.

When one has just seen the woman one loves, the sight of any other woman is a taint; it causes physical pain to the eyes. I can see why.

Man is incapable of desiring by himself: the object of his desire must be mediated by a third element. This third thing is sometimes an exterior object – Don Quixote's manuals of chivalry, Emma Bovary's romantic novels – but it is more often something interior: the being which conjures up desire in the heroes of Stendhal and Proust itself becomes a kind of character in the book. Between the hero and his mediator – vanity in Stendhal, snobbery in Proust – there is woven a subtle tangle of admiration, concurrence and hatred.

With love, it is the opposite of most other passions: the memory of what one has lost always appears stronger than the hope of what one might attain in the future. Yet it is also the case that when we are in love we sense that two steps ahead there is an immense happiness and beyond that the consummation of every desire, depending only on a word, only on a smile.

The spirit of the lover wanders unceasingly between three ideas: she has every perfection, she loves me, how can I gain sufficient proof of her love? But then doubt and delight mingle. The only alternatives are to win her love or to die.

There is always a little doubt to calm. That is what causes the perpetual thirst, that is what makes the life of love happy. Because the fear will not go away, the pleasure never becomes boring. The characteristic of this kind of happiness is its extreme earnestness.

It is uncertainty and suspense that chiefly irritate jealousy to madness. When we know our fate, we become gradually reconciled to it, and try to forget a useless sorrow.

One encounters in the midst of the most violent and unrequited passion moments when one believes with absolute certainty that one is no longer in love; such moments are like pools of fresh water in the middle of the sea. One almost stops taking pleasure in dreaming of the beloved; devastated by her unyieldingness, one finds oneself unhappier still at having lost interest in every aspect of life. Nothingness follows.

People try to reconcile you to a disappointment in love by asking why you should cherish a passion for an object that has proved itself worthless. Had you known this before, you would not have encouraged the passion; but the passion having been once formed, knowledge does not destroy it. If we have drunk poison, finding it out does not prevent its being in our veins: so passion leaves its poison in the mind. It is the nature of all passion: we throw *ourselves upon it at a venture, but we cannot return by choice.*

Is there an art of falling out of love? Pretend that the madness of love has left you and it will leave you. Destroy all her letters and do not read love poetry. No. Love is only vanquished by a succeeding love.

A lone further thought, from a different point of view. *Public opinion: a man in his thirties seduces a girl in her teens. It is the girl who loses her reputation.*

4

When, three mornings later, I finally succeeded in bringing the conversation round to the subject, albeit at an oblique angle, she spoke of the good name of her family.

I was not sure I was going to be able to understand her: on Saturday, she had let a near-stranger pleasure her through her leggings, then by Friday she was worrying, in the manner of some character in a Victorian novel, about the shame that would be brought upon the house. Brought by what? By any public acknowledgement of our intimate relations. I was made to understand that everything must be kept within the confines of my room and the limits of the breakfast hour. It was hinted that there might be future intimacies – 'No promises, mind you' – but only under the appropriate conditions.

She did not appear at all over the weekend. When I asked her on the Monday morning what she had been doing, she would not reply. 'You are not my keeper,' she said.

Each day that next week she brought the tray. She never rushed. When she put it down on the table, she always turned to me and paused for a moment before asking if I wanted the curtains drawn or the tea poured. One morning I would ask her not to open the curtains, in the hope that the relative darkness of the room would help her to overcome her shyness if I could persuade her to come to me again; the next, I asked her to open them, so that I could see her in her full glory. After opening them, she would always pause for another minute. She was a perfectly executed portrait, the window my canvas.

I realized in retrospect that on the mornings before she had climbed into my bed, she had been talkative. Now she was almost silent, sometimes sullen, always demure. She never looked me in the eye. She answered my questions in monosyllables or not at all. When she spoke, she always looked down. This gave her a strange innocence and vulnerability.

She nearly always stood so that I saw her in profile. I took her reluctance to look me full in the face as a mark of her habitual reserve and her shame at the memory of the Saturday morning. I loved her for this modesty. And her profile was of chiselled beauty.

Another weekend when she was mysteriously absent. Or was I worrying about nothing? The weekend routine was that Lizzy should bring in the breakfast and the gentlemen were expected to make their own beds. There was no reason for Sarah to come to me.

On the Sunday, I tried hard to enjoy the company of my son. We wandered around a busy Covent Garden. I was distracted for a moment by the thought of Sarah – that tall, dark-haired girl going towards the tube station, holding her boyfriend's arm: it wasn't, could it have been? I looked down and a gulf opened before me. William the Second was gone.

Blind with panic and guilt, I gasped for breath, looked wildly about me, saw nothing. My punishment, my nemesis. The thought of returning to my wife alone: 'You leave me and then you lose my child, the only person I have left to live for.' I would have to go back and live with her again in order to make up for the loss, perhaps give her another child. And that would mean moving out of the lodging house, losing Sarah. Time went into another of its irregular motions: it felt like hours but in reality it was within a minute that I had seen my son watching a juggler.

I walked over to join him, making myself slow my breathing. I put my hand on my boy's shoulder, just to show him that I was there and that I loved him. I made sure that none of my panic communicated itself. The juggler began with tossing up two brass balls (Which is what any of us could do, I thought) and concluded with keeping up four at the same time (Which is what none of us could do to save our lives, not even if we were to take our whole lives to do it in, I thought). The thought of this extraordinary dexterity distracted my imagination from my imagination of Sarah.

It seemed to cost the juggler no effort.

It was as if it were a mere mechanical deception with which he had nothing to do but to watch and laugh at the astonishment of the spectators. A single error of a hair's-breadth, of the smallest conceivable portion of time, would have been fatal: the precision of the movements had to be like a mathematical truth, their rapidity was like lightning. To catch four balls in succession in less than a second of time, and deliver them back so as to return with seeming consciousness to the hand again, to make them revolve round him at certain intervals, like the planets in their spheres, to make them chase one another like sparkles of fire, or shoot up like flowers or meteors, to throw them behind his back and twine them round his neck like ribbons or like serpents, to do what appears an impossibility, and to do it with all the ease, the grace, the carelessness imaginable, to laugh at, to play with the glittering mockeries, to follow them with his eye as if he could fascinate them with its lambent fire – there is something in all this by which he who does not admire may be made quite sure he never really admired anything in the whole course of his life.

'I liked him,' said William the Second.

'It's all a matter of timing,' replied his father, a tear pricking the corner of his eye.

That night I did some hard thinking. I had got everything out of perspective. I was ashamed at the afternoon's train of thought, the naturalness with which I had said to myself that the worst consequence of losing my son might be the loss of Sarah. She was just a girl, I had never even taken her out to dinner, she was not my lover. I was a father and a writer. I must write to support my son; I must put her out of my mind. I was not only shamed by my thought in the instant I had imagined my son was lost; seeing the juggler had also made me ashamed of myself.

I ask what there is that I can do as well as this? Nothing. What have I been doing all my life? Have I been idle, or have I nothing to show for all my labour and pains? Or have I passed my time in pouring words like water into empty sieves, rolling a stone up a hill and then down again, trying to prove an argument in the teeth of facts, and looking for causes in the dark, and not finding them? Is there no one thing in which I can challenge competition, that I can bring as an instance of exact perfection, in which others cannot find a flaw? The utmost I can pretend to is to write a description of what that juggler can do. Those who cannot do, write. I can write a book: so can many others who have not even learnt to spell. What abortions are my writings. What errors, what ill-pieced transitions, what crooked reasonings, what lame conclusions. How little is made out, and that little how ill. Yet they are the best I can do.

I vowed that I would forget Sarah and become a better writer.

I kept to my resolution, and in the morning was at my desk by nine. Sarah came in with the tray as usual. She was impassive as ever, registering no surprise that I was fully dressed and at my desk, not feigning sleep or sitting up in bed with a book, as I habitually was when she entered. I thanked her courteously, coolly. There was a silence. This was the point at which I always tried to engage her in conversation. I said nothing. She turned as if to go, paused, her profile framed against the window.

'Did you see your boy over the weekend?' It was the first time she had initiated conversation since the Saturday.

I stuck to my vow. 'Yes,' I replied, pleased with myself for turning back on her the infuriating habit of answering in monosyllables.

'How was he?'

'He was fine.' A silence. 'We saw a very good juggler in Covent Garden.' Another silence. 'I thought I might write an article about jugglers.' Still silent. 'And buskers – people who make a living by entertaining passers-by – you know what I mean.' I could not stop the old pattern reasserting itself.

I felt the ends of her hair against my neck. Without my noticing – her silent motion, her *glide* – she had taken a few steps towards me as I was speaking, and now she was standing behind my chair. 'Is that what you're writing now?' she asked.

My heart jumped. 'Yes – do you want to look at it?' She was leaning forward to look at the page, supporting herself by placing a hand on my shoulder. There was another silence. The word 'electricity' filled my mind.

I bent my right arm back across my heart and placed my hand over the hand that was on my shoulder. Neither of us moved or spoke. We both pretended to read the words I had written about the juggler. I took the risk, and with my other hand grasped her by the elbow and turned her on to my knee. Before she could resist – though I sensed that she was not going to – I encircled her waist. We neither spoke nor kissed. She was the mannequin again – but warm.

I began moving my hand slowly, caressing her just above the hip bone. She was wearing a large white cotton shirt, which was obviously a man's. I smelt her neck. My lips found the spot which had ignited her the previous time.

'You'd better not kiss me there,' she said.

'I adore your neck, you know I do, I can't resist it.' So much, I thought, for the previous night's resolution to concentrate only on the writer's art of choosing the best words. Here I was, talking in pathetic clichés again.

Even the most articulate are dumbfounded by love. All tongues are tied. 'I love you', 'I adore you', 'I cannot live without you': tired quotations, the ghosts of lovers past.

'Stop it,' she said, making no effort to force me to stop kissing her neck. Her eyes were closed and I could hear the increasing tempo of her breathing. I moved my hand up to her breast. I had feared that this moment would never return. One of the odd things about being in love, I thought, is the way that the memory of a past touch is the strongest yet most elusive thing. Over the previous sixteen days, no image had been more powerful than that of my hand on her breast, yet I had been completely unable to bring the feel of it back to my mind.

She checked my hand as I tried to undo a button of the shirt. She checked it again as I moved it below her waist. She turned away her head as I made to kiss her. She methodically unwound herself from my arm, got up, and walked out of the room without saying a word. For the rest of the morning I sat with a blank page before me, unable to write a further word about the juggler.

There was a knock on my door at two.

'Yes, come in.' It was her. 'Sarah.'

'You made an agreement with my mother that you would go out for an hour at this time every weekday, so your room could be done.'

'Sarah.'

'You must stick to this agreement. I can come to talk to you in the mornings, but not in the afternoons.'

'What do you mean, Sarah? Don't you see what's happening to us? What have your mother's silly routines got to do with it?'

'I'll come back in a quarter of an hour and do the room if you've gone by then. If not, you'll have to make your own bed today.' And she was gone again.

She's making a fool of me, I thought. I won't play these games. I put on my coat and went out. Instead of sitting in the little square, I walked for an hour, impatient, frustrated.

The next morning I was awake at eight. I could not decide where I should be at nine thirty, in bed or at the desk. Then I thought: I'll show her, and I quietly left the house, not returning till eleven. There was no breakfast tray, but the room was tidy and the bed neatly made. Nobody knocked at two.

When she came in the following morning, she was cheerful and friendly. I was at my desk. 'Where were you yesterday?' she asked. I told her that I had had to go out early to see an editor. 'You ought to tell my mother the previous night if you don't want breakfast,' she said. 'But I took the opportunity to do the room when I came in at nine thirty.'

I grabbed her by the arm and kissed her on the lips. She let the kiss last for several seconds, then pulled away, said, 'Stop it,' and insinuated her way out of the room. It had happened so quickly that I had no subsequent recollection of her taste. I was sad for a moment: my first kiss of the love of my life, and no residual sensation.

When she came in the following morning, her expression gave nothing away. I was sitting up in bed. She put down the tray, left the curtains closed, sat on the bed and put her arms round my shoulders. Her first unequivocal invitation. I plunged towards her lips. Her tongue flickered beneath mine and I felt as if my whole body was melting. She pulled away, pushed me down with a giggle and was in bed beside me, once again with her back to me. We lay still for a few moments, then my hands were moving rapidly over her body; I was holding both her breasts from behind, pushing against her. I moved back a little to let her turn towards me, but she would not. My hand drifted over her buttocks, rested between us on the seam of her denims. Then I tried to take her shirt off. It was white, a man's, like two days before, but this time collarless. She prevented me. There was a struggle; she was giggling, still keeping her back to me. I gave up trying to turn her, and instead worked myself rhythmically against the tight jeans. As soon as I finished, she slid out of the bed. Still she said nothing, but she gave me a half-smile as she closed the door behind her.

5

Over the next few weeks, she brought the breakfast tray
every morning from Monday to Friday. Occasionally she
said that she was in a rush that morning because she had to
do the shopping for her mother. Then she would leave
straightaway. But usually she stayed for at least five minutes' conversation. The pivotal moment was after about ten
minutes. Depending on her mood, she would either leave
with no warning or make the second's eye contact which I
was coming to recognize as the signal that it was a morning
on which she was prepared for intimacy.

Sarah never came to me in the evenings, so I maintained
my custom of going out to eat in the little nearby Italian
restaurant where I had become such a regular that I was
given a special price. On evenings when I was reviewing, I
just had a sandwich before the curtain went up. At weekends there was the usual round of cocktail and dinner
parties among the literary set. I had always hated the small
talk with strangers; now I lost all taste for the salads and
desserts which had been my only pleasures on the dining
circuit. I knew that if I was to keep the work coming in, I
had to remain visible, but all the time my mind was back in
my room. I only wanted to be with Sarah; I was only alive
in the consecrated minutes which began as I awaited her
entrance each weekday morning.

I perfected the art of participating in a conversation

about the latest play, the latest novel, the latest artshow, while thinking of my lovemaking with Sarah. I always regarded it as lovemaking, although we had never technically made love.

It did not obey a regular pattern. The customary progression from liberty to liberty to consummation was not observed. I would never know at what point Sarah was going to stop and slip away. She seemed to have the capacity to turn herself off at will.

To begin with, she always insisted that we remain fully clothed. In case her mother came looking for her, in case she had to go in a hurry, she did have work to do in the mornings, you know. She would be happy to sit up on the bed with me, leaning back against the wall, her eyes three-quarters closed, our fingers intertwined, my other hand working her steadily to orgasm. But she would not let me undo the buttons of her shirt. Once, after she came, she said, 'I've never let anyone else do that to me, you know.' I wanted to ask what she *had* allowed other men to do to her, but that would have spoiled my sense of my own sacred privilege.

One day she told me that she loved chocolates. I did not regard this as a hint, but that afternoon I paid my first-ever visit to Thornton's chocolate shop. I was delighted to be asked whether I wanted my purchase *giftwrapped*. 'Yes, of course,' I replied, thrilled with the little gold rectangular box neatly tied with ribbon. 'I have a little present for you, Sarah,' I said the next morning. She smiled and kissed me on the lips. It was the first time that she had initiated a kiss and the first time that I was the one to pull away for air. Kisses were a special treat, less frequent than other kinds of touch. She said that she had to go, but that tomorrow she might have a little present for me. My work suffered that day.

The next morning she put the tray straight down on the table, turned her back to me and faced the window, but did not open the curtains. She pulled off her sweater and I saw the arched length of her back. I could not stop myself thinking of mermaids and other legendary marine enchant-resses. She was in bed beside me so quickly that I missed the sight of her coming towards me across the room. She pressed herself into my chest. I still had not seen her naked breasts, but I could feel their warmth against me. I found the part of her neck which made her breathing quicken. I sensed her body relax and begin to respond to my touch. I ran my tongue over her shoulder and at last I was kissing her breasts. The hardening of her nipples beneath my fingers had become one of my two greatest pleasures; now when I ran the tip of my tongue over them, she shivered. They were harder then than I had ever felt them; distended towards me. The right seemed a little more sensitive than the left. She allowed me to loosen her belt but checked my hand when I tried to slide it beneath the waistband of her jeans. But when I rubbed the denim at the place where the legs joined, she melted in my arms. She always came to orgasm quickly – I would think back with a mixture of triumph and guilt to the herculean labours of the marital bed – but this time it was the quickest of all.

She once said that she wished she had lived a hundred years ago, so that she could have gone to balls and worn beautiful gowns. I was a connoisseur of print shops and I saw the opportunity to repeat the success of the chocolates, and indeed to raise the stakes a little. The next Monday morning I said, 'I've got a *very special* present for you this week, Sarah.' It was an original hand-coloured engraving of a Regency lady in a ballgown. Sarah looked genuinely pleased; she did not seem to know that such things existed. She kissed me warmly, but again said that she could not stay.

On the Tuesday, however, she took her top off and got into bed beside me. This time she was wearing one of her short skirts. I had noticed as soon as she entered the room that, unusually, she was not wearing tights or leggings. I had often stroked her thigh, but there was always a point at which she stopped my hand, holding me by the wrist, or took a certain upward movement as the cue for the instant termination of proceedings. That morning I knew it would be different. This was the first time that I had felt the naked flesh of her upper leg. I let the back of one hand glide very lightly over the soft skin, while my lips pressed against her left nipple. I felt the tiny hairs stand up. My fingers went higher. She said No, and grasped me by the wrist. I moved my hand back down and caressed her inner thigh for several more minutes, transferring my mouth to her right nipple. I tried again; she said No once more, but in a dreamy voice. And she did not reach for my wrist. I was spreading my touch through the rougher hair and then my forefinger was inside her.

My first thought was: I remember when this finger touched my pen in Paris and I sensed that I would be a writer, not a painter. I went into a reverie of Parisian skies and smells. I was not moving my finger. She was working herself upon it. Her orgasms had previously consisted of nothing more than a single twitch and a sigh, but this time she was panting, gasping for breath. I counted twelve strong spasms as she came. A sense of power and pride stretched me into what felt like a fuller erection than I had ever known. She turned away and let me rub myself against her. There was a silent understanding that I would always ensure I remained inside my pyjama bottoms, so the dampness would not stain her clothes. After she had gone, I remained in bed for a long time, curling myself into the foetal position. I held my index finger against my nose, held it there until I drifted into a delicious half-sleep. It smelt faintly of garlic. That was why I had remembered Paris.

The next week, I was already dressed when she came in on the Tuesday morning. On the Monday I had given her another lady in a ball gown, and my plan was that in return for this we would undress each other. I wanted to take her clothes off myself, to do so slowly, to be in control of the pace of things. I made to lift up her jersey. 'No,' she said, 'let me.' Underneath, she was wearing a plain cream camisole with shoulder straps of a slenderness that made me catch my breath. I thought, again with exaltation but this time without guilt, of the contrast between this garment – its lightness, the freedom of movement it bestowed, the silkiness of its texture – and my wife's wired cages. 'I've got a little present for you,' she said, pushing me to the floor. She was astride me, undoing my fly with a deft (practised?) hand, and for the first time she was touching my flesh, my core. She sat erect, her hair tumbling down all on one side of her head. One of the straps slipped off her shoulder; I could see the outline of her breasts, the flatness between them; I half closed my eyes; I could not remember having ever before concentrated so purely, felt a single sensation so achingly. That day she did not let me touch her.

The third gowned lady did not produce the reaction I had expected. 'They're all the same,' she said. 'They're boring – and they don't even have glass frames, just these cardboard surrounds.'

'Mounts, Sarah.'

'What?'

'They're called mounts.'

'What are called mounts?'

'What you so charmingly refer to as the cardboard surrounds.'

'If you really loved me, they'd have glass frames.'

'You unappreciative little bitch.' I could not believe that I had said it. How had such a remark slipped out? This was the woman I loved more than all the world.

'Thank you for telling me what you really think of me.'

'No, Sarah, no, I didn't mean it.' I was almost weeping.

She was unyielding. But she did not march out – it was almost as if she were enjoying making me suffer.

'I'm sorry, forgive me, I'll do anything, give you anything.'

She allowed my humiliation to be complete. She gave me nothing for two weeks. Each morning I would make an attempt at reconciliation – a word, a gift, a promise – but she would remain cold.

I had a piece of writing to finish, and spring had arrived, so I decided to go down to Wiltshire for a whole week. The change of air changed my resolution. I would forget her, would throw myself into my work, would move out of the house.

On my return, I was cool with her. The resolution lasted but one morning. The second day, before I knew it, without my understanding how it happened, we were in bed together. Exactly what she did next, I had no idea. She had taken off her T-shirt and my shirt, she had pulled down my trousers, and now I could feel her hair and her breasts against my nakedness. Without any pressure, any motion of the hand, I had dissolved, and I was sobbing in her arms as she comforted me like a mother with her injured child.

For over a year, I thought of her all the time, of nothing else. She filled most of my dreams. I fancied that every conscious moment I was apart from her I would be inwardly sharing whatever she was doing. In more lucid moods, I did at least recognize that this was a fancy: after all, I never saw her for more than an hour a day. But still I would be thinking of her. Even in Wiltshire, where I spent many long weekends that spring and summer, she would be in my mind if only because I had determined to clear my mind of her, to be at one with nature and at peace with my work.

The air around her was not like ordinary air. Only to touch her hand was to enjoy perfect happiness and contentment of soul.

I especially loved her when she came in at half past nine looking scruffy, wearing what I regarded as sluttish clothes. Baggy jerseys that slipped off one shoulder; faded denims which tightly hugged her figure and were torn across the knee. When she pushed up the sleeves of her heavy navy sweater, I could not take my eyes off her arms. The only thing I could not abide were her Doc Martens. She once let me kiss her feet, which were small for her height, making it sacrilege that they should be boxed into such heavy shoes.

She said that she had a poor opinion of her own beauty. Her modesty made me adore her all the more. She was convinced that her nose was too large; I thought that it was perfect. 'Is there anything you like about your appearance?' I asked. She admitted that she did like her long hair. She hated wearing it up, though that was necessary for doing the housework and eating spaghetti. I dreamed of taking her to Italy, where I had never been, introducing her to the paintings I loved and to other kinds of pasta, which she could eat with her hair down.

She was once ill, pale, and had lost all her freshness. I only adored her the more for it, falling in love with what I dramatically described to myself as the decay of her beauty. I imagined nursing her as she lay dying in Venice. I told myself that *if she had a sore upon her, I would touch the infection; if she was in a burning fever, I would kiss her and drink the sickness, as I had drunk life, from her lips.*

When she was pale, I thought she was loveliest when she was pale; when coloured by the sun, I thought she was loveliest with colour. When her hair was up, I loved it best up; when it was down, I loved it best down. Best of all I loved it when it was up and she let me unpin it and watch it unfurl. Then she would toss her head.

My blood surged when she appeared in one of her very short skirts or when a turn of the body made it clear that she wore nothing beneath her shirt. But I was jealous of all eyes save my own. The thought of her dressed thus in the street drove me wild. I wanted her like this in my room, but covered from head to foot anywhere else. The thought of another man seeing the outline of her nipples through a T-shirt made me hollow-eyed. I thought that I understood that thing one reads in stories about people literally *tearing out their hair*. Then it would occur to me that it would make no difference even if she were covered from head to foot, even if I flung a chador over her every time she left the house – the grace of her movement as she walked was enough in itself to make all men love her.

Equally maddening was her habit of finding some excuse to come back into my room just after she had left. She would tantalize me a little more, then make off as I was on the point of extracting some new promise from her. I loved and hated her flirtatiousness. It was a sign of her life, but also a sure indication that I could never be sure of her. At times, I found myself looking back with regret on the stability of my relationship with my wife.

She always spoke of our *friendship* and thanked me for my *little presents*. I spoke a different language: 'You move in minuet-time', and, 'I never hear your approach on the stairs but by a sort of hushed silence.'

The mornings I cherished most were those when I read to her, introducing her to poetry. Little gifts of books: a slim selection of Keats, eventually a complete Shakespeare. The collection of my own essays. Reciting and explaining favourite passages, marking them so that she could go back to them in her own time (did she?). It seemed to me that she loved the attentiveness I showed towards her as I read. Sometimes she would sit on my knee while the book lay in front of us on the table; as a treat, she would lie on the bed with me, or very occasionally snuggle in, and I would put my arm round her neck, hold the book on the far side of her head, and see her face at the same time as the page.

On mornings when she touched me, she would leave

with almost indecent haste as soon as I was spent. But once, I held her back and reached for a book.

'I want to introduce you to a new poet, Sarah. And there's only one way to read him – like this.'

'A horny poet, is he?'

'I suppose you could put it like that. Listen. This one's called "The Apparition".'

She gave me one of her looks which I had come to recognize as meaning either, I don't understand the word, or, What is he going on about now?

'An apparition – like a ghost.' And I pulled the white sheet over my head. Crisp bed linen was one of Mrs W.'s stronger points. Sarah relaxed: playfulness seemed easier for her to deal with than lovers' talk.

' "When by thy scorn, O murderess, I am dead," ' I began, ' "Then shall my ghost come to thy bed . . ." '

She shivered when I reached the poem's final threat. 'It's cold in your room this morning,' she said.

'So what did you think of it?'

'I thought poems were supposed to be about love, but this bloke hates his girlfriend.'

'Maybe she's given him reasons to hate her. Or maybe it's just a defence mechanism on his part – he's afraid to lose her.'

'Well, he's not going the right way about keeping her.' She disentangled herself and went to the mirror to straighten her clothes. 'I must go, I've got things to do.' And pausing at the door: 'He's not my type, that one.'

I did not try any more John Donne. Shakespeare she found difficult, but Byron she loved. After a while, *Don Juan* was the only poetry she would let me read to her. She understood it and found it funny, sexy, sad. She liked the way the women in the poem always seemed to know and to get what they wanted.

'Why else do you like it more than all the other poems we've tried?' I asked.

'Because there's not so much fancy language' – Rose's phrase, I remembered – 'and the people in the book seem real.'

We both thought for a moment. It was Sarah who continued: 'The way you talk about books, it's like you're only interested in them for their own sake. You're always going on about what one book says about another book, not what they tell you about life. You're a critic, aren't you? That's just books about books.'

I could not think of a reply. Sarah, meanwhile, could not be stopped: 'I mean you know all this stuff about dead writers from long ago and far away, but what do you know about the people all around you? Like the man living in the room opposite yours?'

My mind was a blank.

She pressed me: 'What's his name?'

'Follet, isn't it?'

'Right – so what's his job?'

'I don't know. I've never really talked to him. We say good evening.'

'Exactly.' She ruffled my hair and left the room.

She's a witch, I thought, she's robbed me of the power of speech. As soon as she had gone, all my arguments came back to me – it was not true that I did not attend to ordinary people, I had more time for the folk in the bar of the Wiltshire inn than for Elder's academic crowd.

As was always happening, the thought summoned up the image of an open book. I had only read the words once, but they were ingrained upon my memory: *You will hear more good things on the outside of a stagecoach from London to Oxford than if you were to pass a year with the undergraduates, or heads of colleges, of that famous university; and more home truths are to be learnt from listening to a noisy debate in an alehouse than from attending to a formal one in the House of Commons.*

My old friend and intellectual sparring partner had come to mind because I was due to see him that evening. We went out for a meal together about once a month; Elder had (predictably) become a lecturer in philosophy at the university.

That night I tried out Sarah's argument for myself: 'Don't you sometimes feel removed from life, spending your days going through the old philosophical puzzles which have been around since the time of Plato? I mean, for the practical purposes of day-to-day living and loving, who needs a formal philosophy?'

'Billy-boy, I sometimes think you've not listened to a word I've said about philosophy since that absurd lecture I was foolish enough to take you along to. We gave up on the old questions donkey's years ago – the good life, the mind–body thing, and all that. They're no-go areas. Whereof we cannot speak, there must be silence. What we do now is analyse the rules of the game. You must have heard me talking about ordinary-language philosophy. Anyway, what's this about *living and loving*?'

I was annoyed with myself for letting the word slip out. I did not want to tell my friend about Sarah. Elder, who had

never married, always spoke clinically about his relation-
ships with women. 'It's a simple contract,' he had once
explained, 'always made explicit before anything happens.
One, no involvement while I'm still teaching them. Two,
what I offer them is a certain extension of their education
and what they provide for me is a certain energy and
athleticism. Three, no emotional involvement, no strings. It
works every time.'

If these were the rules of his game, he would not begin to
comprehend my willingness to play by Sarah's rules. It was
best to change tack.

'You know what I mean by living and loving – our old
argument about the human capacity to become another.
Whatever anyone says, I still think that's the value of books
– to make us see through eyes not our own.'

'You dear old-fashioned thing,' said Elder. 'My colleagues in the English department would hoot to hear you
say that. No professional theorist of literature believes in
that education-for-life crap any more. A text is just a system
of signs. Not that these deconstruction people know how
to conduct a philosophical argument.'

'At least we agree about something,' I said. I did not care
for modern literary theory.

That night I could not stop thinking about Sarah's
scepticism regarding the value of books.

*The learned pedant is conversant with books only as they
are made of other books, and those again of others, without
end. He parrots those who have parroted others. He can
translate the same word into ten different languages, but he
knows nothing of the thing which it means in any one of
them. He stuffs his head with authorities built on auth-*

orities, with quotations quoted from quotations, while he locks up his senses, his understanding, and his heart.

Sarah only once gave me an evening. I took her to the theatre. Like true lovers, we sat in the dark on the deep red seats, holding hands. I revelled in her pleasure in the playing, her unformed but wonderfully intuitive understanding of the nature of good acting. As we walked back afterwards, it became apparent that her judgement of each performer was exactly that of the professional critic. I was as impressed by this as I was touched by her worry that she might lose her coat in the theatre. Pressing her hand as the lights went down for the second act, I knew that this would be my happiest-ever night in a theatre. I remembered nothing of the production.

But then there was a period when I was afraid to go to sleep because every night I had the same dream. *I woke up with her lying beside me, but she was a corpse, cold, without a heart.* Tea, which had once been my daily pleasure, had lost its flavour and its moisture.

Some mornings she would rub herself against me for a full hour. I loved the frown which fell upon her forehead in the final seconds before her climax.

The memory of the first morning when she had come to me was stronger than the hope of consummation, yet still I longed for some further turn, some further experiment. But I never pressed her to go the final length. I liked thinking about the distance we still had to travel; I liked the idea of the object still to be attained. Her averted eye was a measure of my continuing desire.

In Wiltshire there were moments of a kind of peace when I wondered whether perhaps I was no longer in love –

though I had no idea what could take the place of being in love. Then came moments when I convinced myself that she *did* love in return. And then the doubts. I played squash for a whole day to try to clear my body of desire, but to no avail.

She hated it whenever I used romantic language. 'Don't get sentimental with me,' she would say again and again. If I ever tried to make plans or share my dreams of our future together, she would say, 'Why can't you go on as we have done, and stop using the word *forever*?'

Once, when the house was empty, I went up to the top floor, where I knew the family had their rooms. The first door I came to was half open. I looked in and knew it was Sarah's. I had never seen such an untidy room: crumpled tops and underwear on the floor, a dressing table covered with little perfume bottles, empty lipstick tubes, oils, cleansers, buds of cotton wool, stubs of eye pencil, a locked diary (if only), a heap of earrings, an open jewellery box with beads spilling out. The bed was unmade. Cassette boxes were strewn over the floor; I knocked over a pile of tapes beside the radio-cassette player the noise of which had often disturbed me as I tried to work in the evenings. She had her own little television; on the wall were posters of film stars, hunks from advertisements, singers. The three gowned ladies were face down on the floor beneath the dressing table; the books I had given her – except my own, which I could not see – in an uneven heap in the corner.

I did not tell her that I had been to her room, but the visit gave me some ideas for little presents, or 'petits cadeaux', as we now called them – I was teaching her a few phrases of French, had told her that if she had been a lady in an earlier time, this would have been one of her accomplishments. Perfume, a pair of earrings, a gold heart-shaped locket on a chain, which she let me place round her neck from behind (she then let me put both hands over her breasts, also from behind – her flesh seemed cold that morning). I refused to descend to giving her tapes by her favourite pop stars. 'You don't call them pop stars,' she said. 'They're rock musicians.'

This precipitated us into a blazing row about heroes. I fumed about how the age of heroes was gone, told her of how disgusted I had been at Père-Lachaise, where the young made their pilgrimage to the grave of some drug-crazed pop star whilst I had stood musing over those of Proust, Bernhardt, Balzac and Géricault. She said I was a pretentious old git. I said, 'At least I believe in things that last more than three minutes.'

'Yeah, dead things, dead heroes,' she returned scornfully. She tried to persuade me that the lead guitarist of her favourite band was a great artist. I found it difficult to argue with her, all her bands sounding the same to me. Besides, rational argument was impossible with her: she would get bored, she would change the subject, she would run the back of her hand over my lower stomach, she would leave the room.

According to her mood, rows of this kind, which as the months passed became increasingly frequent, ended either in her marching out or in our bodies working rapidly against each other, fingers dug hard into each other's backs. We often argued about whether anything could happen in the afternoons; she never agreed that it could, but the argument itself would provoke ardour in the morning hour. Before meeting Sarah I had hated scenes; now I loved them.

Sometimes the rows would make me desperate, but more often they caused me to stiffen. She knew how to get the reaction she wanted. Once she accused me of regarding her as nothing but the nearest available body. For the next week, I only talked to her of books and paintings, made no attempt to touch her. But then she said it was my body that she liked, not my words and my work, and, knowing this meant she was ready for me again, I leant back and let her hands wander over me. I felt young and strong.

One morning I went to look for Mrs W., in order to tell her that I would be going down to the country for a long weekend. She was not in the kitchen, so I ventured up to the top floor for only the second time. The door next to Sarah's had a little stick-on plaque announcing that it was Lizzy's Room. So I went to the far end of the corridor. The door was ajar. I was about to knock when I heard a low sighing. Curious, I pushed it slightly further open. I was looking straight at a full-length wall mirror. The bed was reflected in it, and on the bed I saw the familiar figure of a woman in her forties. Her eyes were closed, she was panting now. Her parted legs stretched towards me from the mirror, her skirts were raised and the motion of the hand beneath the knickers made the material ripple as if a crab were wriggling inside it. I crept downstairs, dazed. What was the line – Gertrude's? Goneril's? – about the difference between man and man?

O the difference betwixt mother and daughter. Unless.

6

The Complete Card

Sometimes, especially when in Wiltshire, I examined myself
honestly. On such occasions, I was forced to acknowledge
that there had been pricks of doubt from the start.

Increasingly, I challenged Sarah about her past, the other
lodgers, her evenings, the weekends. She said that she never
let any other man do to her what she let me do, that I was
the only one with whom she had a special friendship,
special morning conversations. But the doubts grew. Often
I heard her return late at night; sometimes I thought I heard
her giggling in the street outside in response to a male voice.
I wondered about Griffiths, the drunken Welshman, but
could not believe she could stoop so far.

In the autumn, a few weeks after I had completed my
first year's residence, the middle-aged man called Follet,
who always said good morning or good evening, but never
another word, moved out. Sarah came in one morning soon
after to announce that someone had shown interest in the
room opposite mine. 'He's called Mr Tomkins,' she said,
'Doing his articles for the law.' I did not like the animation
with which she delivered the news – especially since I knew
that Sarah's older sister had made what the family regarded
as a very good marriage to a now fully qualified lawyer
who had been resident in the house when doing his articles.

Tomkins moved in about ten days later. He was ten years
younger than me – ten years closer to Sarah – and he was

handsome in the most conventional way. Tall, dark hair, strong profile, straight back. Come to think of it, a male version of Sarah. She always claimed that she had no interest in *looks*, but I did not believe her. I discovered that Tomkins's chosen breakfast time was seven forty-five. I was not usually awake by this time, but now I set my alarm clock for seven-forty and listened for Sarah's footsteps.

It seemed to me that within a matter of days the time between the knock on Tomkins's door and the sound of it closing for a second time and the footsteps descending the stairs had increased from two minutes to five to ten to more. I thought I heard low voices, giggles and then silences. Worse still, I was convinced that Sarah was continually finding excuses to go to Tomkins's room in the evenings. She had never once been to me after dark.

I challenged Sarah.

'I never spend more than five minutes in any room but yours.'

'I hear you going to Tomkins and staying a full half hour – longer.'

'That's not true, you're imagining things. That's typical of you.'

'What can I do to make you love me alone?'

'I don't love you, I just like your conversation.'

'And the things we do together.'

'And the things we do together – but if you keep getting at me like this, we won't be doing them any more.'

Sometimes when she let me touch her again, I thought that all was well and that I had been imagining everything. But when I tried to make her look me in the eyes while denying that she gave any favours to Tomkins, she refused.

Then I comforted myself with the thought that she never looked me in the eyes anyway. Then I wondered why she never looked me in the eyes. *I felt the alternate ascendancy of different passions, the entire and unforeseen change from the fondest love and most unbounded confidence to the tortures of jealousy and the madness of hatred.* I wished that the play I had taken her to see had been *Othello* instead of *Romeo and Juliet*. Then she would have known what was in store for her.

The only hope of possessing her, of keeping her from the arms of my rival, was to marry her. Now there was an incentive to divorce. Impulsively, I arranged to meet my wife. She saw no reason to change the current arrangement; it was satisfactory to her and best for William the Second. I insisted, threatened. But what threats were available to me? She had the boy and she had more money than I did.

'Do you seriously think I'm going to divorce you for some chit of a girl?' she asked with what seemed to be genuine incredulity. 'I've seen you "falling in love" before – your infatuation will have passed in a month and you'll see what a fool you are.' I heard her mutter, 'Jane Baugh writ large.'

Fresh-faced Jane Baugh. I'd seen her a few times down in Wiltshire; I had only been joking when I told my wife that I had fallen in love and, later, that I was desolated by the news that the girl was engaged to a local farmer.

«« »»

A day and half a night of solid writing. Names, faces: almost there now. Sally Shepherd, Fenella Gifford, my missing Sally, Jane Baugh, Sarah (whose first word in my arms was Jane). I must, however, still be confused, because try as I may to find my wife's full name, all I can think is Sarah Stoddart.

Or is that so impossible? Samuel Taylor Coleridge was married to a capable woman called Sara Fricker but madly and dejectedly in love with the passionate Sara Hutchinson.

7

I returned to the question each time I saw my wife after taking William out for the day. Her answer was always the same. A remarkably level-headed woman, all my friends had said when we married – not the sort of person you would have expected William to fall for. I was beginning to despair.

I discovered that the law gave me no ground to divorce her. Two years' separation with consent was my best hope, but she would not consent, so there could be no divorce until we had lived apart for five years. I knew in my heart that Sarah would not wait five years for me, that I had to have her soon or I would lose her for ever.

How the matter of my divorce would end – when my wife would agree to it, the financial consequences, the effect on my son – I could not say. I did not care except as it affected my relationship with Sarah. All that I desired was to have it in my power to make her an offer of marriage directly and unequivocally, to see how she would take it.

It was the first day after the New Year's holiday. For sixteen months Sarah had been my obsession, my life. She brought up the post with my breakfast. She recognized the handwriting of my wife, but said nothing. She tantalized me – for no more than ten minutes on this occasion – then left me to eat my leathery toast, drink my cooling tea, and read the letter from my wife. Quite unexpectedly, it announced that since a full calendar year had passed, she was willing to divorce me.

But there were two conditions. I would have to do so in Scotland, since that was where we had married (the little chapel in the Borders, the smell of pine). The Scottish courts worked in a different way, so we would need Edinburgh lawyers. And secondly, she still would not agree to a petition on the grounds of two years' separation with consent. It would have to be on the grounds of adultery – that way, I would have to pay her court costs. The sting in the tail of the letter: 'And it will, of course, be necessary to name the co-respondent.'

I was angry. It was a trick, nothing but a ruse to blacken Sarah's name. But then I thought: Sarah cannot be named as my partner in adultery, for I have not committed adultery with her. I have never committed adultery – though if it makes me free for Sarah I am quite willing to be publicly proclaimed as someone who has. I wrote back to my wife directly, thanking her for agreeing to let me go and asking if she would consider dropping the condition that the woman be named before the court. But she was not in the mood to compromise: if I wanted an immediate divorce, those were her conditions. And if she was going to be forced to file a petition, it had better be one that would stand up in court. She would not have me pulling a fast one halfway through the proceedings in order to get out of paying the costs. The adultery would have to be provable.

By this time, I was in the mood for a fight. If we were going to play it the old-fashioned way, I would make a proper job of it. I explained to Mrs W. that I had to go north on business and might be away for three or four weeks. I decided not to tell Sarah my plans. On my return I would surprise her with the glad news.

I had recently written three pieces for one of the better-paying papers, so I had a little more money in the bank than usual. I withdrew all of it. Dealings would be in cash. I took the train to Scotland and went straight from the station to the first lawyer's office I could find.

The workings of the Court of Session were explained to me. I in turn explained my twin dilemma: that adultery had to be provable, but that I did not want Sarah involved. Was there a possibility that once my wife knew that I was serious about proceeding with the divorce she might name my love out of spite? The lawyer explained that the only cast-iron proof was to be caught *in flagrante delicto*. As for the possibility of Sarah being named, an inference of adultery could be drawn if one spouse were proved to have shared a bedroom for the night with a third party (*if only*, I thought, and remembered that the same two words had come to me on the only occasion when I had been in Sarah's bedroom). An inference would not necessarily be drawn, the lawyer continued, in the absence of other evidence of mutual passion, merely from propinquity, opportunity, or evidence of familiarities. I turned over the words: there had been propinquity and opportunity almost daily for over a year, there had certainly been familiarities. But the wretched thing was that the passion had not been mutual. Still, it was some consolation that this meant that Sarah could not be implicated. I would take responsibility for the rest.

I checked into the cheapest, seediest-looking hotel I could

find. The smell of damp; linoleum; loudly patterned yellow wallpaper; pink nylon bed covers. It had to be done in the appropriate environment.

I went to the roughest-looking pub I could find. I got the information I needed.

For two days I was unable to act upon it. Hard as I tried to be a good actor, I could not stave off the self-disgust. It would be such a betrayal of Sarah, and of William the Second. I bought a bottle of whisky. Unaccustomed to drinking, I found it easy to anaesthetize my conscience, my finer sensibilities.

I went to a different pub, sawdust on the floor. The first man I approached with the offer of some easy money almost killed me. The second had an accent so thick that I could not understand a word of it. The third agreed immediately in a slurred voice; realizing that the man was too drunk to be reliable, I extricated myself, again narrowly avoiding being throttled. The fourth was a little younger than I would have wished, and to my further humiliation regarded the whole thing as a bit of a joke, but he understood what was involved. He had greedy eyes, which was a good sign: the danger was the possibility of selecting someone who would take the ten pound 'advance' and never be seen again. When this lad saw the further ninety which I said would be his if he did what was required, he was hooked. He did not demur at my request for evidence of an authentic name and address: without further bidding, he flipped open his wallet and showed his driving licence. I informed him of the address of the hotel, the room number and the time he should appear there. I also extracted an agreement that if for any reason things went wrong that night, a further advance of ten pounds would be passed over, and there would be a return visit at the same time the following night.

Just before midnight, I made my way to the district; fortunately, it was close to my hotel. I knew that I had to gain agreement in advance because a name and address would be required. First I established the going rate. Then I saw an older woman whom I thought would be a good bet. She swore and shouted when I made my proposal. I began to worry – if it had taken four attempts to find a man who would agree, how many would it take to find a woman willing to take the much greater risk? And how long did I have before the police might turn up?

Then in the shadows I saw a tall black girl. From the way in which she hung back, I had a suspicion that her skin was not to the taste of the average Edinburgh punter, and that she usually had to wait for the other girls to be picked up first. Already in the few minutes I had been there, two girls had been taken away in cars, one escorted on foot. Although my senses had been wholly numbed by the whisky I had drunk first in my room, then in the pub, my head was clear. It was a cold, windy night. Surely she would be glad of a couple of hours in the warm.

The first step was achieved: she looked as if she believed my assurance that I was nothing to do with the police. But having crossed that hurdle, I was not sure that she fully understood. I repeated the conditions over and over again: three times the going rate, in return for being discovered, giving her name and address, and no subsequent denial. I repeatedly reassured her that there would be no court appearance. She pushed me to four times the rate; I agreed in return for an advance glimpse of the evidence of her name and address. She said she would have to get her child allowance book from her room, which was nearby. I waited at the foot of the stairs, afraid that she would have second thoughts and I would never see her again. Time crawled. I must have looked at my watch over a hundred times in the ten minutes before she returned. She looked as if she had smartened herself up a bit, put some lipstick on. We walked quickly to my hotel.

Everything had gone according to plan. It was going to cost more than I had reckoned on, and I had not even begun to pay for the lawyer; a bank loan would be necessary, but the writing had been going well and I had not been in the red for some time, so I was fairly confident of my bank manager's co-operation – and Sarah was worth every penny.

Once in the room, I knew that I could no longer postpone addressing the one question I had kept setting aside. How serious was my wife about the 'proof'? Could I risk a situation where I and the girl and the young man all perjured ourselves? Surely she would not push it this far; surely it would be enough to give the date, the names of the hotel, the witness, the girl? But the whisky reminded me of my vow that if I was going to do it, I might as well do it properly. My sensibilities were, I kept telling myself, anaesthetized. It would not be as if I were actually touching her, betraying Sarah: I had bought a packet of condoms in the pub just in case. Sheathed, it would not be my true self. My self would be held in by the tight band and could then be flushed away as if it had not been given. It would not be as it had been with Sarah when that self had flowed freely (though she had always been careful to prevent it coming into contact with her). I hardened slightly with the memory. Then another worry: would it actually be possible after all the whisky?

The girl was undressing. Involuntarily, I looked away, as Sarah always made me. It occurred to me for the first time that there was something odd about Sarah's refusal to let me remove her clothes. I stirred again with the thought of her nakedness. The girl was silent.

I would not go near her head, feeling revulsion at the idea of lip contact. But I was excited by the blackness of her skin. Sarah's long black hair, I kept thinking, Sarah's long black hair. But then I was brought down by the smell of the cheap perfume she had applied when she went to get her child allowance book.

'Come on, love,' she was saying, 'we won't fit it on unless you can do a bit better than that.'

The hired witness, the greasy-haired youth, was in the room. Was he early or had it taken longer than I had reckoned on to find the girl?

The girl was panicking, raising her voice. She seemed to have forgotten the conditions and was imagining she had been inveigled into some weird act of voyeurism or troilism. 'Just fucking forget it, you pervert,' she sobbed.

The boy wasn't helping: 'She's not bad, is she? I wouldn't mind giving her one myself.' And after a pause for thought: 'Tell you what, I'll knock twenty quid off if you let me.' The girl raised her voice in protest; I tried to hush them both, concerned that the hotel proprietor or the occupant of the next room would shortly be joining the bizarre party. I told them that if they did not keep quiet, the whole deal would be off. The youth said, 'Watch it, mate, I reckon the two of us could take you on,' and he winked at the girl. She was getting dressed.

'Slow down, slow down,' said I. I had put my dressing gown on now, and was seeing clearly again. I held out a pen. 'Here are the prepared statements, just sign, and you'll have your money.'

'What's to stop this bastard robbing me of mine?' asked the girl.

'Fuck off, whore,' came the reply.

'Easy, go easy,' said I. There was a kind of authority in my voice now. The others were quiet for a moment.

'Just sign.'

'But we didn't do it.'

'Doesn't matter – just sign and you'll have the money.'

I counted it out. The sight of the crisp English ten-pound notes did the trick. I was sure I heard them bargaining in stage whispers as they went down the stairs.

I threw open the window to clear the room of its cocktail of foulness. I did not sleep till after five, did not wake till lunchtime. The rest of the day passed in a hungover haze.

But I felt better the following morning. The deed was done, and I had barely touched the girl. In the cold, clear air of Edinburgh, moving from morning to night like an automaton, I dealt with petitions and preliminary financial proposals.

At last an evening came when what I described to myself as my 'dark night of the body' was sufficiently distant for me to feel ready to write to Sarah. I also thought a lot about what turn my other writing might take in the months and years ahead. A comic novel about sex, perhaps? I had some material now. If only I were not so earnest about love.

After setting the divorce in motion and before returning to London to propose to Sarah, I spent a few days in the Highlands. I wanted to clear my head of the marriage and the business, so that when I went to Sarah my only thought would be our future together.

I had always loved walking, could go for twenty or thirty miles a day and be off again the next morning, fresh as ever. The Shropshire hills of my youth; the Wiltshire lanes; once the Vale of Llangollen. I liked to walk alone. Talking was for the town, walking for getting out of town. To walk was to be at *liberty* in the highest and fullest sense of the word. The clear blue sky overhead, the green turf beneath the feet, seven or eight unencumbered hours, and then to thinking. *The undisturbed silent eloquence of the heart.* Plunging from the sight of a cloud into my own past being and reveries of the future. If the side of a mountain was grassy, I would bound down it in huge strides.

The road followed the very verge of the lake. It was hard, level, rocky, with low stone bridges periodically flung across it, and fringed with birch trees, just then budding into spring. Behind the trees, as through a slight veil, I saw the huge shadowy form of Ben Lomond. It lifted itself directly from the edge of the water without any projecting lowlands; in this respect, I thought, it had a great advantage over Skiddaw (my father had loved walking, too, and in his last years I had sometimes taken him for long weekends in the Lake District; he had remained remarkably fit; I had told him that Wordsworth climbed Helvellyn on his seventieth birthday). I tried composing my walk into an essay. *Loch Lomond comes upon you by degrees as you advance, unfolding and then withdrawing its conscious beauties like an accomplished coquette.*

The scene was all water, earth, sky. I was free, I would be free for Sarah. I would bring her here; she would run, *free as the mountain wind.* Ben Lomond commanding to the right, the Trossachs beyond, tumbling about their blue ridges like woods waving. Lower mountains to the side; round pastoral hills, green, fleeced with herds, and retiring into mountainous bays and upland valleys, *where solitude and peace might make their lasting home – if peace were to be found in solitude. One image alone haunted me amidst the mountains, turning all the natural beauty to a mockery and a dream.*

Before taking the train south from Waverley station, I called in on my lawyer. The petition had been lodged; the co-respondent was 'an unnamed woman'. My wife obviously thought that she had won the game of bluff. I felt mildly triumphant: I had got what I wanted without infidelity to Sarah.

My lawyer also handed me an envelope with a London postmark. My heart leapt: the handwriting was not my wife's, so it must have been Sarah's (I had addressed my letter to her from care of my lawyer, not the hotel). Her handwriting was neat, schoolgirlish; her spelling was far from perfect; the letter was of a single page, thanking me for mine and saying that all the family and lodgers were well. I read it over and over, trying without success to decipher the emotions that lay beneath its surface. But she had written, that was what mattered. I returned to London with high hopes.

As the train pulled into King's Cross station, I thought I sensed the air thicken with the consciousness of being near her. As I approached the house, my stomach churned. I unpacked with the door open, in the hope that she might walk past.

She did. She paused and greeted me, but I saw at the first glance that something was different. I pressed her to come in and talk. She declined. She stood in the doorway, cold, distant, averse. She refused to answer when I asked if she was displeased with me because I had been away, whether she was not glad that I had returned. When I stepped towards her, with the obvious intention of kissing her, she literally tossed her head and walked away.

The next morning, Mrs W. brought the breakfast. 'Just to make sure you're settling back in.' I stayed in at my two o'clock time, but again it was the mother who appeared. I barely slept that night.

I recognized Sarah's knock a little after half past nine. As she put the tray down, I asked her if she was altered since I had gone away.

'No.'

I had decided not to mention Tomkins by name. Instead I asked indirectly, using the novelettish language in which we had sometimes played, if there was anyone else who had been so fortunate as to gain her favourable opinion.

'No, there is no one else.'

What was it then? Was it anything in my letter?

'No, nothing.'

'Your reply seemed a little cool.'

'That wasn't its intention.' If I wouldn't mind excusing her, it was her busy shopping morning.

I convinced myself that she was just performing her usual act of tantalizing me. In another day or two she would be back in my arms and I would be able to tell her that I would soon be free. But she did not bring my tray the next morning.

It was a Friday, and I was due to see William the Second on the Sunday, for the first time since the trip to Scotland. I would have to tell him about the divorce. My wife, I was sure, would not have mentioned it to the boy: it was my responsibility. Usually I took my son out for tea or a burger after we had been to the park, the zoo or a museum, but I thought that on this occasion it would be better to bring him back to the room, in case there was a scene. I knew that my boy would hate to be seen crying in public. I asked Mrs W. if, as a particular favour, she could provide afternoon tea, with some special cakes, on Sunday. I would of course pay extra. She said that it would be a pleasure – Sarah would bring up something nice for the boy, and there would be no question of an extra charge.

I did not tell William about the impending divorce. Instead, as we stood feeding the ducks, I explained that I had a special friend at the place where I was staying. But my special friend was angry with me. Did William the Second think he could do anything to make her like his father again? William the Second said that he was not sure; William said that if William the Second was very nice to her over tea, that might do the trick.

Sarah looked sulky as she turned into the room with the tea tray in her hands, but her expression changed the moment she saw the boy. She asked if she could stay for a while and talk to him. I sat in the chair by the desk, while the girl and the boy knelt on the floor eating fairy cakes, playing noughts and crosses, and talking about pop music. Afterwards, William the Second said, 'I had a lovely day, Dad – I wish we'd been back to your place before and met Sarah. She's great.'

In the morning, Sarah said, 'You've got a lovely boy.'

Before I knew what I was saying, I replied, 'Would you like to be his step-mother?'

She laughed and said, 'Don't be so stupid.' And she kissed me.

In an instant we were wrestling on the floor. I was burying my face in her hair. She was taking off her clothes. She seemed less shy about her body. I had never seen her properly before, never been able to gaze at her as I had gazed at the nudes in the Louvre and the Jeu de Paume. I was kneeling over her, drinking in the lines of her body. The angular shoulders, the small round breasts, their nipples erect with pleasure or cold, the flatness of her stomach, the contours of her legs. I went down to kiss her feet as I had done once before. I stretched out my hands and grasped the one remaining garment.

'So you want everything off,' she said. For once she did not resist. It was the only occasion on which I was ever allowed to remove any item of her clothing. I was kissing the dark place now, extending my arms and massaging both her breasts as I did so. It was finished in an instant, a few strokes of the tongue and she was rolling away from me.

We lay in silence. I was fully clothed, she was naked. I noticed for the first time that her buttocks were slightly plump.

'You could do the same for me,' I said.

She sat up, her eyes blazing. 'I had an attachment once before, but that person never attempted anything of the kind.'

The novelettish language made me smile. 'An attachment?'

'Don't laugh at me,' she said. 'It's not funny.' She was putting on her clothes. 'Just forget it.' The atmosphere was suddenly that of the Scottish hotel.

She was gone. What had been my mistake? To ask, rather than to wait for her to offer? She kept changing the rules. I also had a suspicion that she might have backed off because of my little hint about the possibility of a marriage proposal. Her initial reaction had been to reward me with her nakedness, but she had then made sure that there would be no afterglow of vulnerability and intimacy in which I could tell her that the divorce was underway and that I would soon be free for her.

I could not get to sleep that night. I tossed and turned for an hour, trying to comprehend her. Towards midnight I went downstairs to get a glass of water.

Fragments of conversation in the kitchen. It was not a Wednesday night, but Caj was there – a special occasion, perhaps a birthday or anniversary? The family were in high spirits. The mother's voice was loudest, but the older sister was there too (though not her husband?). Lizzy was presumably in bed and the father was either absent or silent.

'Follet wore a surgical support.'

Gales of laughter.

'Griffiths is a prize specimen.'

'If those trousers were to come down, what a sight there would be.'

Caj's voice: 'What do you suppose then? Seven inches?'

Mrs W. (to whom I had mentioned my embarrassment on the landing that first September Saturday): 'He's quite a monster – our writer friend nearly tumbled over it one night.'

More gales.

Then Sarah's voice.

It did not matter what she said; it was enough that she was there.

«« »»

What is the point of denying it now? It does matter what Sarah said.

She said: 'Closer to eight, if you ask me.'

«« »»

When I began reading the classic novels as a teenager, I decided for a week or two that I would make a career out of dramatizing them for television, bringing high narrative art to a wider audience. People who usually read only pulp fiction would watch the televised version, then go out and buy the original.

Sometimes my conversations with Sarah seem doubly distant. It is as if they were spoken not by me and her, but by two characters in a film – a film set not in the present but the distant past.

Possible dialogue for the screenplay of a costume drama?

Interior. Morning.

W. You are angry with me?

S. Have I not reason?

W. I hope you have; for I would give the world to believe my suspicions unjust. But, my God, after what I have thought of you and felt towards you, to have the doubt cross my mind – that you might be a common lodging-house decoy, your lips as common as the stairs.

S. Let me go!

W. No – prove to me that you are not so, and I will fall down and worship you. You were the only creature that ever seemed to love me; and to have my hopes and all my love for you turned to a mockery – it is too much! Tell me why you have deceived me, and singled me out as your victim?

S. I never have, sir. I always said I could not love.

W. Do I not adore you – and have I merited this return?

S. I have repeatedly answered that question. You sit and fancy things out of your own head, and then lay them to my charge. There is not a word of truth in your suspicions.

W. Did I not hear the conversation downstairs last night, to which you were a party?

S. I had rather not hear it!

W. One word more. Did you once love another?

S. Yes, and ever shall most sincerely.

W. Then, *that* is my only hope. If you could feel this sentiment for him, you cannot be what you seem to me of late. Kiss me, you witch!

S. Never.

W. Then go, but remember I cannot live without you.

She leaves, with no visible reaction upon her face.
He throws himself on the bed.
He throws a few books, papers and clothes into a battered
canvas knapsack.

Cut.

Exterior. Mailcoach setting off from Piccadilly.
Horses paw the ground. Outside passengers sit erect.

Cut.

Exterior. Man with knapsack walking down country lane
towards half-timbered inn.
English pastoral music.

8

My letter from Wiltshire was filled with the kind of words that fill all such letters.

I cannot live without you. It is not what you say or do – it is yourself I love; to be with you is to be at peace, I have no other wish or desire. Far in the future, when all your other lovers have forsaken you, I will creep into your arms and die. I cannot bear the thought of having lost you for ever. I ask myself how long one can wait for love to be requited, and the answer is for ever.

No reply. I yearned for the pleasure of seeing her handwriting again. She had, after all, sent that cordial, if brief, reply to the letter I had written from Scotland. It was my dearest possession. It did not matter to me that I was a writer and that she could not spell.

It did not matter to me that she had been present during the seven-inch conversation. I had gone back upstairs, dazed. I had lain on the bed, numb. I had convinced myself that I could still hear their laughter. They were probably discussing my own dimensions.

But that was just the influence of the mother and the brother. Nurture not nature. Take her away from the family and she would be the angel I knew she had it in her sweet nature to be. I would still ask for her hand.

I returned from Wiltshire with complete determination.

In my old-fashioned way, or perhaps because I was

conscious of the difference of class, and uncertain of the conventions of her kind, I spoke to the father first.

I had always rather liked Mr W., who quietly read his newspaper as the wife flapped and gossiped around. I liked him still more for his abstention from the seven-inch conversation. I felt sorry for him: he had probably been tricked into marriage by the voracious woman (whose hand had looked like a crab as she pleasured herself).

It took several attempts to get him alone in the family parlour, a room I hardly ever entered, save when I had to settle my account or inform my landlady that I was going to Wiltshire for a few days and so did not require breakfast.

There seemed little point in working round to it slowly, beginning by talking about the weather. Oddly, we found ourselves each calling the other *sir*. I had a fleeting memory of the old black-and-white films my mother and sister used to watch on the television on Saturday afternoons.

'I'm sorry to trouble you, sir, and I fear this may come as something of a shock – but I want to marry your daughter.'

Mr W. put down his newspaper, paused and collected himself. There was a dignity here that was altogether lacking in the mother. 'I had half-suspected this, sir, for I have to tell you that once I walked past your room on a morning when I was off work and I saw the intimacy between you. If I am not mistaken, Sarah was sitting on your knee.'

An embarrassed silence. It was the father who broke it: 'I am glad, at any rate, that your intentions are honourable.' Was this his natural idiom, or was he speaking the language he thought the middle classes spoke? Perhaps we were both under the influence of the films, quoting the stereotypes because we were afraid to be ourselves.

'I have to confess that intimacy, as you call it, of that kind has continued between us almost daily for over a year.'

The father seemed genuinely shocked. 'I take it, then, that this proposal is forced upon you by, by – her condition.'

It was a moment before I understood. When the penny dropped, I was adamant, angry. 'No – nothing could be further. . . .'

Mr W. was both relieved and apologetic. He said that he didn't have any say in the matter – Sarah was approaching her twentieth birthday – but that he'd be pleased to have her off his hands. She didn't really earn her keep doing the housework.

I was not exactly elated, but I supposed I could not have asked for anything more.

The proposal was equally clumsy. It turned into a kind of debate, an act of persuasion. The very fact of its being a word-match doomed it to failure.

'You take pleasure in my conversation and you say you have an esteem for me; it is upon this, after the honeymoon, that marriage chiefly turns.'

She said that she would never marry a man she did not love beyond all the world. It did not occur to me to ask where she had found the fine turn of phrase. Films, romances.

The old argument: if she did not love me, why did she come to my arms? If, as she claimed, she never went to another man's arms, then surely she loved me.

She said that she had no other tie.

My relief: 'You are not going to be married soon?'

She said that she did not know where on earth I had got that idea. She had no intention ever to marry at all.

Desperation: 'Could you not come and live with me as a friend? You always speak of our friendship.'

A mumbled evasion. My heart pounds, for this is not an outright refusal. But then she says that it would be of no use if she did, for I would always be hankering after what could never be.

Anger: 'Why do you treat me thus? What have I done to become so hateful to you?'

Her coolness: she has always told me she had no affection for me.

'But I adore you.'

She did not want adoration.

'Can't you at least be friends with me as of old?'

She could give no promises.

'Will you make your own terms?'

She would make no bargains.

And, as so often, she was gone. She always got the last word.

I sat blankly at my desk.

I had no sense of how much time passed before there was a quiet tap at the door. I started to my feet, tipping the chair back so that it fell against the bed. She had changed her mind, she was coming to her love!

It was Lizzy, with a pile of books. 'Sarah says that in the circumstances she thinks she should return these.'

Numb, I looked at the spines. Every book I had given her except my own. Another of my moments of hope: she has kept my book, the copy I inscribed to her, this must mean that I have some small place in her heart, that all I need do is persevere.

'No, no, no,' I said vacantly. 'She must keep them all.'

'The thing is,' replied the child, 'I don't think she wants to keep them.'

'Well you must keep them then.' And I gently pushed her out of the room.

I was not sure whether it was over or whether it was just another turn in the game. Perhaps she would come in the following morning and offer to return my own book; I would insist that she should keep it, whatever the future might hold; she would say that it was her most prized possession and once again I would behold her naked. Perhaps then we would finally go the last length.

All that day I longed to go downstairs and ask her to accompany me to Wiltshire, where I would make her my wife. We would live in a cottage with a wood-burning stove and cornflowers in the garden; I would cultivate raspberries and Sarah would learn to paint.

But something withheld me. In the evening, however, I could not rest without seeing her. I went down. Lizzy was in the hall. 'Do you know where your sister is, Lizzy?'

'She's gone out.'

'Do you know where?'

'To my gran's, I think.'

'Where does your grandmother live?'

The girl looked surprised, a little uncertain as to whether or not she should reply.

'I meant it when I said that you must keep the books for yourself,' I added. She told me the address.

Lizzy was a good girl, I thought. Prettier by the day, too.

She must have turned fourteen by now; had taken to wearing a bra. A budding grove. I remembered my first kiss: Fenella Gifford had been fourteen. Come to think of it, Lizzy had the same pixie face. Let Sarah go, stay in the lodging house, educate the younger girl who still had some purity in her . . .

I checked my *A to Z* and set out. It was not far away, and it was easy to work out which way she would be coming if she were on her way home. I passed a house where I had once rented a room and had not gone much further, ruminating on chance and change and old times, when I saw her coming towards me. I felt a strange pang at the sight, but I thought she was alone. Then some people in front of me moved on, and I saw another person with her.

The murder was out.

It was a tall, good-looking young man, but I did not at first recognize him. We passed, walking in opposite directions across a side street.

After all that happened over a period of nearly two years, after all that had happened in the previous few months, after what had happened that very morning, she walked past me without even changing countenance, without expressing the slightest emotion. She had had no time to prepare for acting a part, to suppress her natural feelings. I thought: the truth is, she does not have a single natural feeling to suppress.

I turned and looked; they also turned and looked. Then, extraordinarily, as if by mutual consent, we both retrod our steps and passed each other by a second time in the same way.

I returned to the house. I was stifled. I could not stay in

my room. I walked into the street and met them coming towards the house. A third time she walked past me, her face impassive.

I walked the streets for an hour, two hours. My head was both full and empty.

I returned to the house around midnight. At the top of the stairs, just as I was about to unlock my room, the opposite door opened. I saw that Sarah was not inside, though I could have sworn I caught a faint whiff of her distinctive garlic smell.

Without having time to prepare for acting a part, I asked Tomkins – in a hushed voice, so as not to wake the house, and in the decorous tones of a rival lover in an old novel – whether he could spare a few minutes' conversation on a subject that was highly interesting to myself and, I believed, not indifferent to him. We went into my room.

In the course of four hours' conversation, it came out that since three months before my departure for Scotland, she had been playing the same game with us both. Tomkins breakfasted first and enjoyed an hour of her company, and then I took my turn, so we never got in each other's way.

Tomkins was astonished to discover that Sarah's intimacy with me had continued after his own arrival, and indeed right until the present. She had assured him that there was nothing between her and the more long-standing lodger, save occasional polite conversation, just as she had assured me that there was nothing between her and the new arrival. She had merely hinted to Tomkins that she was unable to give him her whole heart, her whole self, because she was still attached to a former lover.

Tomkins had pressed her with regard to the other

lodgers. She had been implacable on the subject of myself – there was never anything more than talk. She lingered over my breakfast because she was interested in my writing, that was all. She did, however, admit that she had for a short time had 'a bit of a thing' with Griffiths, the Welshman. 'But nothing serious,' she added, 'and it was all over very quickly.'

We had both been fed the same phrases. 'Never stayed more than five minutes with anyone but you.' 'Determined to keep every other lodger at a proper distance.' Her self-possession through all the fondling was manifest proof (Tomkins's phrase, the rising lawyer) that it was her constant practice.

It was clear to us both that the mother was in on it too.

Sarah no doubt reported every detail back to her. And she would touch herself, her hand moving like a crab, in rhythm with the thought of Sarah playing with me, Sarah astride Tomkins, Sarah stroking the massive Griffiths.

It was all a device to make the lodgers stay, to humiliate us, and ultimately to make good marriages for the daughters. It had worked with the older sister and Lizzy would be next in line.

After a while, we stopped talking about Sarah. It was too painful: the hurt of her infidelity coupled with the shame and embarrassment at the idea of the family laughing at us. We talked instead about ourselves. Our own families. Our past loves, our work, our hopes and fears. For the first time, I opened my heart on the subject of Sally.

Sally, my student love, with the red ribbon in her hair, the little lines down her cheeks when she smiled, the one damaged tooth. How we had been carried away on the first night and her period had then been late, so I proposed to her, and then her period came, but we agreed that we would marry anyway, and I spent all that was left of my student grant on a solitaire diamond ring, and I loved her with all my heart, and two months later she slept with another boy from the art college, a boy I had thought was becoming my best friend.

How I then had some sort of a breakdown, but recovered in Paris. How from then on I shielded myself with the armour of my work. How I had my books and my poetry to protect me – until I was punctured by Sarah. Crumpled armour.

«« »»

'Sometimes it was Sarah and sometimes it was Sally.' Sally's age then was Sarah's age now. Was Sally a dim prefiguration of Sarah or Sarah a distant echo of Sally? It all depended on whether you found yourself by delving back into the past or setting out towards the future.

«« »»

Tomkins put an arm round me. It was four o'clock in the morning.

In the cold morning light, conviction glared in upon me *not only that I had lost her for ever, but also that every feeling I had ever had towards her – respect, tenderness, pity – all but my fatal passion, was gone.*

I left a blank cheque for Mrs W.: 'You have been good to me, I trust you to fill it in for the appropriate amount.' I wondered if she would comprehend the irony of both the words and the gesture.

I caught the first train out of King's Cross.

On the train I thought back to the terrible scene towards the end of my foundation year.

'I can't believe you've done this to me, Ben.'

'These things happen.'

'I thought you were my friend. All that talk about brotherhood in art.'

Blond, tousled Ben Haydon. He and I and Sally had drawn each other and been drawn to each other. We were the only ones in the group who regarded our course as a vocation rather than a training. For me, though, the bohemianism had been but a pose; sharing our ideas, sharing our art, had not meant sharing Sally.

It had been Ben I had blamed then, not Sally. But this time I bore no ill will against Tomkins.

In fact, I had to admit that I liked the young lawyer. Although obviously incapable of my own intensity of passion, this was a man who genuinely seemed to love. I would not have felt any resentment towards *him* if Sarah had announced that she was carrying Tomkins's child and would stay with him for the rest of her days.

«« »»

Two memories strangely elided: a happy child in the family home, being given a lesson by his father as his older brother sketched the domestic scene. And over the image, her words, 'I always told you I had no affection for you.'

9

I had to return to Edinburgh in order to tie up the final particulars of the financial settlement which went with the divorce. The Stoddart woman had driven a hard bargain, but for the sake of my boy I felt bound to accede to it in every particular.

The advantage of going north again was that it put as many miles as possible between me and Sarah. I could not bear to be apart from her; I knew that if I remained in London I would be drawn to the lodging house, would loiter round the door waiting to torture myself with a glimpse of her on Tomkins's or some new gentleman's arm.

Edinburgh was as before – grey, windswept, bitterly cold. As so often, my memory furnished me with a description lodged from my reading. I did not know – and was too tired to bother about – to what extent the place took its atmosphere from my state of mind, from my reading, or from the true weather conditions.

Stony-hearted Edinburgh, what are you to me? The dust of your streets mingles with my tears and blinds me. City of tombs, a quarry rather than the habitation of men. Your cold walls reflect back the leaden melancholy of the soul. The square, hard-edged, unyielding faces of your inhabitants have no sympathy to impart. What is it to me that I look along the level line of your tenantless streets and meet perhaps a lawyer like a grasshopper chirping and skipping, or the daughter of a highland laird, haughty, fair, and freckled? I turn instead towards the promontory that reaches into the sea; it is the beacon of my banished thoughts, pointing the way to my heart's true home. The air here is too thin for me; all air is too thin that is not enriched by her sighs.

I could not bear to let my gaze rest on the brisk Scottish girls; the sight of any female save Sarah positively pained my eyes. A single visit to my lawyer and a few signatures finalized my business.

Another blank here. No recollection even of the accommodation or the weather. Long letters to old acquaintances: the catharsis of *writing* about her. A last wild plan conceived and executed. The agreement reached, the date set, the faint hopes and the fearful imaginings. Through the late summer, I idled away my weeks. All I was waiting for was the letter from Elder.

I wrote bitterly in my notebook, then threw the notebook away.

What chance is there of the success of real passion? What certainty of its continuance? Seeing this as I do, and unravelling the web of human life into its various threads of meanness, spite, cowardice, want of feeling, and want of understanding, of indifference towards others, and ignorance of ourselves; mistaken as I have been in my public and private hopes, calculating others from myself, and calculating wrong; always disappointed where I placed most reliance; the dupe of friendship, and the fool of love – have I not reason to hate and to despise myself? Indeed I do; and chiefly for not having hated and despised the world enough.

One evening I thought I was returning to life. I bumped

into a Scottish literary editor for whom I had written some of my longer, less journalistic essays. I had often spoken to him on the telephone and once met him in the flesh at one of the many London launch parties or exhibition openings that over the years I had attended out of professional necessity, at which I always drank Perrier water and stayed for as short a time as I decently could. I introduced myself and was told that I was not looking at all myself, that I had aged, was thin, my hair scattered and my cheekbones projecting cadaverously. I would not have been recognizable, but for my voice and my smile. It was exactly this directness which made the tall Scotsman – Jeffrey? Miller? (why won't the memories wear name badges like the hospital staff?) – the most astute, admired and feared editor on the literary scene.

We spent several hours together getting slowly drunk and arguing with equal portions of amicability and heat. I remembered my old spars with Elder, how we would talk through the night and I would walk home in the dawn light of London's only quiet hour, exhilarated, intellectually punch-drunk.

Our conversation turned to the eighteenth century and the Scottish Enlightenment in particular. Each of us in a different way saw himself as an inheritor of that tradition of robust iconoclasm. We circled around the old argument about whether men were governed by their passions more than their interest or reason. I of course argued for the passions. But my companion maintained the contrary: 'The *main chance* is the great object in life,' he proposed. 'Look round the pub here – every man, however passionate he may be about his particular hobby or obsession, minds his business as the principal thing. What we're all ruled by is the endeavour to make both ends meet at the end of the financial year.'

It was a shrewd and very Scottish argument, I thought. I replied that I knew plenty of people who had been ruined with their eyes open by some freak passion, some whim or fancy. 'I know someone who married a girl he knew was an airhead, someone who's drinking himself to death, someone who falls for every fast-buck con, someone who divorced his wife to marry a tart at a lodging house who refused him and whose cruelty and charms are the torment of his own life and that of all his friends. There's another who's the slave to his wife's ill humour, another who quarrels with all his friends without any motive, someone else who lies on to the end of the chapter and to his own ruin. Where's your calculation of consequences there? The pleasure or torment of our lives is in the pursuit of some favourite passion or perverse obsession.'

As we parted the editor said dryly that I certainly had the more passionate, if not the more reasonable, argument. I returned to my lodging with a certain elation, not wholly attributable to the fact that I had broken my golden rule and drunk alcohol. In the morning, however, I was left with nothing but a sore head. There was a fat envelope for me with a London postmark.

The letter was cast in the form of a journal.

10

Sunday 4th September. Went there and asked for room, as you said. Mrs W. very communicative – mentions daughters – says gentlemen generally stayed two or three years – a Mr Crombie was in the front room that long. From what you told me of the layout, I think the room I've got was that of Tomkins; your smaller one seems to be empty.

Monday 5th. Move in. Am taken to the family parlour (didn't expect this, from your account). Meet the girl, about to go out (to meet one of her lovers, eh?). You are mentioned by Mrs W. – her 'famous' gentleman. You famous?! The girl looked as if she had been on the point of going out immediately, but found excuses to linger when I was in the room. Took her coat off and put it on again.

6th. Mrs brought up the breakfast but Miss came up to take the tray. Happened that she came in as I was dressing. She didn't seem at all embarrassed, so I thought I'd waste no time. She repulsed the kiss very gently. She was back and forward all day, finding any excuse to come into the room. She *expressly forgave* the freedom I had taken! I asked if there was a newspaper or book I could borrow and she brought up your essays. Signed copy, eh, Billy-boy?

7th. She brings breakfast. Nothing happens, but she offers to bring tea at eleven o'clock, I ask for coffee, she brings tea, smirks, backs out of the room and returns ten minutes later with coffee and 'apologetic' grin. Said she was on her way out for a couple of hours. I told the mother that the bed hadn't been made; she said Sarah had said she'd made it. S.'s lie, so she had a reason to come up to my room again on her return?

That night, late, I went down for a glass of water. The brother was in the kitchen – Cal? Caj? – said he stayed over one night a week. Said you always drank water and tea, never beer or wine. 'Unlike Griffiths.' Said you were a 'queer fish', 'jumpy'. Said – smiling – you were in love. Didn't ask with whom, but manner and tone convinced me that the whole was a regularly understood thing, and that there was nothing singular about a 'gentleman' being *in love* in that house.

8th. Got a paper and lent it to the father to read. Saw Miss several times. In the evening, pressed her to stay for coffee in my room. She declined, but I followed her to the door and kissed her several times on the stairs, at which she laughed. Had hold of one of her hands, the other was at liberty but she did not once attempt to raise it so as to make even a show of resistance. What was that phrase of hers you quoted in your letter setting this business up? 'Being determined to keep every lodger at a proper distance'?

9th. This time I insist she drinks coffee with me; say I will not sit alone, am not used to it, and that if she doesn't stay, I won't have any coffee at all, will take my hat and walk out. Awed by this terrible threat, she agrees to stay. I sit on the bed, ask her to sit with me. She says – wonderful delicacy! – that she'd rather sit on the chair. Door is ajar; I shut it to keep out the draught. No objection. I think I hear footsteps – guess the younger girl has been watching on the stairs and is now going down to announce the new

arrangement to the rest of the family. That other phrase
you quoted? 'Never stayed more than five minutes with
anybody but you'? She pours the coffee and the talk
commences. Ask which of the pieces in your collection is
her favourite. She seems at a loss. Say I think that the one
on racquet games is good. Ask what she thinks of the
remark about being 'twice young' when playing the game.
She says that you were 'full of your remarks'. Ho, ho. Ask
what else she's read – does she like poetry? Says you'd read
her something with some funny rhymes, but she'd found it
rather rude. Did she like the theatre? Yes, you'd taken her
once, but she'd never been to the opera. Hint that she'd like
to go. Moving up-market? To be honest, Billy-boy, she's
quite incapable of understanding any real remark. After a
while, she just shut up, for fear of being found out for what
she is, a little mawkish simpleton. Some of the things you
say she said to you: I'd say they were just stupidity, not
deliberate put-downs. What the hell were you doing with
her, William? For god's sake, you almost had the makings
of a philosopher when we were students. She got up to go
after about ten minutes, but when I pressed she remained for
another quarter of an hour. Then said she must go to her
sister's to bring Lizzy home. A lie, because I'm sure it was
the little girl's step on the stairs. I kissed her and let her go.

10th. Saturday. Lizzy brings breakfast. The family like
me because I pay attention to them all. Talk to father about
what's in the paper. They invite me down to the parlour for
the evening. Sit opposite her and then next to her. She said
little, but laughed and smiled and seemed quite at her ease.
I brushed against her a couple of times. No objection to the
familiarity, even in company. She's got strange eyes – brown

but somehow with no colour to them – motionless, glassy. I reckon that's why she's always looking down – she knows her eyes are her worst feature. To be honest, Billy-boy, she's no great beauty. Frankly, the mother's better built. On rising to go upstairs, I saw a little pile of books. Obviously presents from you, now left around to make the family seem cultivated. Mrs W. asked if I wanted one to read in bed, I said I thought I'd better not as I wanted a good night's sleep. Mrs W. gave accord, but said she'd send Sarah up with one in the morning, so I had something to occupy me on my lonely Sunday. Clearest evidence that the mother's in on it.

11th. She brings the books up. I ask her where they're from. You, of course. I ask her which was your favourite. She says the Shakespeare. Did she remember any passages you especially liked? Yes, there was one you had left a special mark in. She turns to it. I read – Florizel wishing Perdita a wave of the sea. I look at her as I read and she is perfectly unmoved. Says she has work to do. I pull her to me and kiss her on the lips. Her tongue responds and she does not pull away when I put my hand on her tit. Then she goes. She brings up coffee in the evening but says she can't stop as there is nobody in the house but her father. Prick-tease.

12th. Brings breakfast as usual. This time I'm at the desk writing (writing this to you, actually, but I cover it up when she knocks and scribble a logical proposition on a blank sheet of paper on top of it). She puts down the tray and leans over me, asking what it is I'm writing. I pull her on to my knee, slip my hand up her little skirt. Rather a plump thigh. Play with her neck-band and work my way down into her bra. Rather small breasts. She untwists herself just before I make it into her knickers. Ask her if she'd like to go to the opera. If I get a pair of standby tickets, we could be lovers tonight, I remember thinking. I mean that I could bed her. Couldn't ever imagine her as a *love*, since she's got no conversation in her. There's a lot to be said for girls with degrees.

13th. No luck with the opera tickets, but got her between my legs this morning. Right into contact. No resistance or complaint, but again pulls away when my hand is on the point of slipping in. I feel flirtatious, like never before – 'I'll kill you with kissing, if I catch you,' I say (uncharacteristic, I know). She grins, 'But you must catch me first,' and she bounds downstairs, looking up laughing from the bottom. Little vixen, she really needs to be given one. Christ, did I say that? – what's going on here? You did ask me to tell you *everything* that happened.

14th. She doesn't come up in the morning. But in the afternoon she's in to make the bed. I grab her and say I'll give her a good tickling for her trick in running away from me yesterday. Get my hand between her legs. She says, 'Let me go.' Pushes me away, finishes making bed carelessly (but no *blush*). Did you notice how it is that *she never looks at you*? I say that I'm sorry and that I'm lonely. She says that she has to go, but that if I'm lonely she might be able to come and sit with me one night when everybody else has gone to bed. But no promises.

15th. She didn't come last night. I didn't sleep. I can't believe I'm letting it affect me like this. The mother brings the breakfast. I only see Miss once in the day, when I chase her upstairs, tickling her between the legs from behind all the way up. She's giggling and breathless at the top, but won't come into my room.

16th. Saw nothing of her in the morning. Saw her later, asked her to bring me coffee. Said she 'never drank tea or coffee with the gentlemen'! She was altered in her manner. Went out in the evening. On way back, saw her leaving the house by herself. Followed her – asked to accompany – she refused – on my offering to take her arm, she stood stock still, immoveable, inflexible. I felt defeated (that I should admit this! – you never defeated me in all our nights of argument). She's a hard one, Billy-boy. Like a gentleman, I said I wouldn't press her. I offered my hand. She shook it, looked me in the eye, and went on to her lover.

First thing in the morning I pay the mother for a month and leave. Don't bother to reimburse. Just don't ever ask me to do anything like it again. You take care of yourself now. A.E.

11

The test had gone the way I had dreaded and known it
would. The last desperate hope gone. What hope? O, I
don't know – that Griffiths was an aberration, Tomkins a
true lover, my own advances tolerated out of pity or because
she was flattered. But that she could have gone so far with
Elder in just ten days.

And now Elder was clearly in love with her, damn him,
damn her. A classmate I had regarded as a friend.

Everything was as I had feared. My rational mind had
been telling the truth all along, but my struck heart had not
let me hear. My love had been an insanity. It had been
entirely a condition of my own creation, a form of brain-
fever. The artist had been allowed to make half-love to his
creation, but not to possess it wholly. She was nothing but
a coquette; she had done the same thing with all the lodgers
and she was prepared to go as far as they asked. Worse, she
was neither especially beautiful – 'frankly, the mother is
better built' – nor remotely intelligent. Her beauty had been
in my eye alone.

I had hardly ever seen her in the company of others or
away from the room where I had fallen in love with her.
Save when we had been to the theatre, and the pleasure of
her being mine for the evening had meant that I was too
happy to take in her appearance, I had never seen her out
of doors. With Sally I had walked in the park; we had run

hand in hand with rain trickling down our necks. My love for Sarah had been confined to a single room, the air drawn from it by the gas fire. I thought of my last sight of her, in the street, arm-in-arm with Tomkins. She was not as tall as I had remembered her standing or lying in the room. She was not as beautiful. One would not have *looked twice* at her in the street.

My dreams of initiating her into the world of poetry and painting, of being to her as the exiled professor had been to me, were hopeless delusions. She had not even read a single one of my essays, probably had not even opened the book (save to look at the inscription of her own name).

On my earlier trip to Scotland, I had written to her of my work, saying that I was anxious to do well now, because I wished her to hear me well spoken of. My stomach turned with the realization that she did not have the capacity to appreciate my work. In all probability she despised it and would have admired me more if I had been a skilled joiner. I remembered one of the draining conversations in which I had tried to persuade my wife to divorce me: 'You have always despised me and thought little of my abilities.' Her devastating reply: 'Are the women with whom you associate now any better judges of your work?'

To have given up my boy and my wife for this. The irony of 'timing': I had first come to Scotland to begin the divorce proceedings, had returned in triumph, ready to tell her I was free, only to be greeted by the seven-inch conversation. The irony of the fact that the last thing she wanted was a marriage proposal. And now I was back in Scotland, the divorce complete. No son, no home, no money, not even the dry wit of the Stoddart woman.

And worst of all, no illusions, no pure memories. The test had seen to that. I missed my son, my cat. I missed my wife. For a frenzied moment, I wondered if I could go back to the lawyer, halt the settlement, reverse the clock. Perhaps the anguish was really to do with the divorce and the loss of my son. Sarah was just a pretext. What was the psychoanalytic word – sublimation? But I did not want to go back to my marriage; I wanted to go back to Sarah's arms.

Sublimation: perhaps she had once been hurt herself, and now she was taking out her pain on the rest of the male sex. Perhaps I could go back to her and take the pain away.

Numb, holding Elder's journal-letter in my hand, I walked out of the dreary boarding house, not even stopping to put on my coat. I walked through the streets, having no idea where I was going. I walked briskly, passers-by must have thought purposefully. But I had no purpose. I walked for hours, four miles, eight miles, twelve, out of the city, into the dusk. In the night I was stumbling along country roads. I sat in the dark for several hours shivering by a wall, still holding the pages inscribed in Elder's neat, superior hand.

In the first light of dawn I walked on, west and north. I had left the letter on the dewy grass by the wall. My mind was whiting out now, as it had done in the days after Sally when I had stayed up all night poring over the philosophy books. I knew that I had to walk away from the south, away from the light of the morning sun – the same sun which had twinkled through my curtains on that August morning some two years before, the first sunny morning after the dull weather of my first week in the lodging house.

But I began to forget what else it was I was walking away from.

I was off the road. A loose-stoned track wound through a wood. I heard a river below. I wanted to see the water, its bright cleanness in the weak morning sun. A few steps off the path, the top of a steep bank studded with a few rocky outcrops.

All I could think of now were odd phrases from Elder's letter. It maddened me that I could not remove the words from my head, could not burn them out of my thoughts. My mind would not stop being imitative.

Her lips as common as the stairs.

I was back in school. The set text was *Henry the Fourth*. 'This Doll Tearsheet should be some road.' The teacher was laboriously explaining the joke – she was like the common highway, so many men had gone over her. The dirty laughter of teenage boys.

As cold as a statue, as hot as a whore.

The unremitting *vulgarity* which Elder had mercilessly documented.

Choose a mistress from among your equals – those of an inferior station to yourself will doubt your good intentions – they will be ignorant of the meaning of half you say, and laugh at the rest.

Do not imagine you can save the people whom the politicians have abused and deserted by choosing one of them, raising them up in your own image.

She would not have understood the first thing about Eluard and heroic resistance; in Père-Lachaise, she would have followed the crowd and accepted a joint. I cursed the indescribable weakness of mind to which she had reduced me.

Fragments, voices.

She never once betrayed herself by any momentary forgetfulness, by any appearance of triumph or superiority to the person who was her dupe, by any levity of manner in the plenitude of her success; it had been one faultless, undeviating, consistent, consummate piece of acting. Which fool of love was this?

Why had I not realized it all along? Why had I not listened to the warning voices. She had once said, 'I defy anyone to read my thoughts.' I had replied, 'Do they then require concealing?' But I had not stopped to ask myself what it was that she might be concealing.

Then the memory of a morning when I had woken up gasping for breath after dreaming that I had lost her. *Can I breathe away from her?*

The truth that I never had any pleasure, like love, with anyone but her.

The night I had all but blocked out when, sleepless, wondering how long I would have to wait for news from Elder, I had left the boarding house and walked the streets, found myself back where I had negotiated the farce of the staged adultery, and taken my pleasure with the girl who looked most like her, but who grinned horribly, whose skin smelt and was streaked with a rash. But even the whore, I believed, would have grown fond of a man who returned to her so incessantly. The whore would have developed a certain tenderness, a kind of motherliness unknown to this monster.

Her heart seared, her eyes gloating with habitual hypocrisy and lech for the mere act of physical contact. The bitch wanted a stallion not a lover. Running mad for size. All she wanted was to be touched and go all lengths but the last, to be thrown on the floor and felt and all and still resist and keep up the game.

Doing it with every man who entered the house, going different lengths according to how she is inclined that particular day, that particular hour. With Tomkins at eight-thirty and me at nine-thirty.

She never wanted to marry me. *All she had was an itch for being slabbered and felt.* Once the itch was relieved, that was that, thank you very much, sir. But what I had wanted was to possess her soul, to fuse my being with hers. When my itch was relieved – by her, by myself – I felt worse than ever. For two, three seconds I would melt and be – like the actors I admired – beyond myself. Then nothing, then disgust.

That first Monday morning when she came to my room: as she went out, she turned round at the door, with that inimitable grace with which she did everything, and fixed her eyes full upon me, as much as to say, 'Is he caught?'

That first Saturday morning when she came into my bed: I could not see her face as I brought her to orgasm, but I know how it would have looked as I touched her – hungry.

And when she touched me? Bored.

I probably could have had her in the *sporting-line*. Griffiths did, Elder could have done. But I loved her far too much to think of that: I was glad that we never went the final length. We were saving that till we were together for ever, in our little cottage in Wiltshire.

Her words when I challenged her the morning after the terrible conversation: 'I always said I could not love.'

The only thing that soothes me is the idea of taking my little boy whom I can no longer support and walking through the country as beggars. But what if he were to ask after my special friend Sarah who had spent a happy teatime with him talking about music and playing noughts and crosses?

She always spoke with finely turned, polite sentences, never malformed ones broken by the vulgar interjections of her class, 'like' and 'you know'. Was that part of the act too, since she knew I was a man whose craft was words?

Often my fondness for her made my heart ache. It was tenderness, not sex, for she was the daughter I never had. My little sister who died after the Atlantic crossing.

Hating and loving at one and the same moment.

What have I done these last six months?

I have sat day after day, evening after evening, I have lain night after night, crying my eyes out, my weakness growing upon me. I have had no hope left save that I could lose my senses quite. I think I should like that – to forget, ah! to forget – there would be something in that – to be in oblivion for twenty, forty years and then to wake up a poor wretched old man, to recollect my misery as past, and die.

The last letter to her, to which there was no answer, not a line.

The rolling years of eternity would never fill up that blank. Where shall I be? What am I? Or where have I been?

The bank falling away beneath my feet. A glimpse of the river in the gully, but the eye caught by the sun on a blue-remembered hill, sweeping me into the far distance.

The slenderness of her waist.

12

Sunday morning. Sunshine.

So that is who I am. *So have I loitered my life away, reading books, looking at pictures, going to plays, hearing, thinking, writing on what pleased me best. I have wanted only one thing to make me happy; but wanting that have wanted everything.* O Sarah. Sarah Jane. When shall I burn her out of my thoughts?

Laura was right. The recent memories have come back and they are fuller by far than the earlier ones were. They feel almost complete. Only a few things are missing. Some special token that was noticed, discussed, given, returned, broken, mended. Had she said that the figure reminded her of a former boyfriend?

But it is the first of the returning memories, the fragments and glimmers of the more distant past, that I yearn for as I look back on what I have managed to catch with my pen. I shall discharge it, and then myself. In the recent memories there is too much that is trivial and too much that is painful.

«« »»

There are always more visitors in the ward on a Saturday. Yesterday afternoon came a small, smiling girl, perhaps in her mid-twenties, with auburn hair, darker at the roots. She lit up the room. She was wearing a black T-shirt on which was emblazoned in French 'It would be better to dream

253

your life than to live it, save that to live it is also to dream it.' I could not take my eyes off her for the hour's duration of her visit. It was the only hour of the day or the night when I was not writing.

After she left I felt a momentary disloyalty to Sarah, but it took only another moment to lay that down. The girl was like the first breath of sea air on my childhood holidays. We used to arrive at teatime and before going to bed would walk down the road to the clifftop. To smell the brine, to anticipate the morrow.

I am ready. I have worked it out for myself. I will not deny that Laura helped, but I do not need her any more. There is no reason to tell her what I have found. No reason even to seek an official discharge.

Sunday means a skeleton staff and half the patients out for the day with their families – I will not be missed until nightfall and I will have made many miles by then. They know that I walk after lunch. I know my way around the grounds. One fence to climb, then the woods and the hill beyond. No possessions to take with me. I have learnt to write again, so I can start my life again.

I will begin by returning to Paris. On the first day I will go to the Louvre. One of the patients has told me I will find it altered: in the courtyard they have built a glass pyramid, which everyone admires, and the entire collection has been rearranged. Did I not dream of going back and asking for the old pictures – and not finding them, or finding them changed or faded from what they were? And crying myself awake. I might look for the painting of which Sarah's face and hair reminded me the first morning I saw her. But that is not especially important to me. I do hope, however, that I will not have difficulty in locating the painting monkey.

I wonder how my French will have been affected by the amnesia. Among the books I want to rediscover are some which need the sound of their own language.

Another voice, that of a different fool of love, tells of how he wrote a book called *Love*. The girl never yielded to him, never loved or understood him. He saw her for the last time; the next year he published his book of love; three years later she died and he wrote the date of her death in the margin of one of his own copies of the book (he said it found only seventeen readers in twelve years) and he wrote beside the date in English, though he was French, 'death of the author'. Should Sarah then be acknowledged as the author of my book, my life?

Perhaps in Paris I will meet the dead author. We will walk in the Luxembourg gardens together. Like two excited children, we will hire little sailing boats, squat on the edge of the circular pool and push them out with the wooden rods. Then we will walk round and round, comparing notes. I will be able to discover which of the fragments and aphorisms about love are mine and which are his. I will tell him about Sarah and he will tell me about his beloved – Mathilde? Marianne? Names are still a struggle.

I begin to have a relish for life. I am looking forward to the things that I like: the motion of cats, salads with red and yellow peppers, the view of Rydal Water from the Loughrigg terraces, the smells of new-mown grass and baking bread (I am at ease; I can forgive myself the cliché), cornflowers in all colours but especially blue, a firm bed, incorrigibly held but undogmatically articulated political principles, buttered toast with very bitter marmalade and the crusts cut off, landscapes by Poussin, raspberries, aquamarine and burnt ochre, a fountain pen of my own, crème brûlée, essays and meditations, cricket and squash, Souchong tea, every note of Mozart, wood-burning stoves, Cézanne, Sherlock Holmes, films by Louis Malle, trains, *Flaubert's Parrot* and other stories told in double time, walking in light shoes on the lanes and footpaths of southern England, Woody Allen, the arrival of the morning post, Wenlock Edge on a hazy June morning, Roland Barthes (especially his lover's discourse, his book on Michelet which interweaves his own words with those of his hero, and certain passages in *Roland Barthes par Roland Barthes*, which I like because the narrator is sometimes 'I' and sometimes 'he').

I am even looking forward to the things that I don't like: small dogs, overweight women in slacks, marigolds (Sarah's favourite flower), the early afternoon, landscapes by Claude Lorrain (classical perfection but no energy), strawberries (Sarah's favourite fruit), loudly patterned wallpaper, biros, fast food, unnecessary words (*like* and *you know*), Living Flame gas fires, Cubism, the actress playing Lolita in Stanley Kubrick's otherwise excellent film, London traffic, the realist novel, the dinner-party circuit, making telephone calls, post-structuralist intellectuals with the exception of Roland Barthes, scenes.

I will start going to films again. I cannot wait to recapture the magical sensation of the moment when the audience is stilled and the first few frames establish a whole new world into which we all sink in a delicious oblivion, a fantastic projection.

Another voice, that of a different fool of love, asks whether a memory is something you have or something you've lost.

But I am still uncertain as to whether these memories I have written are truly mine. How will I ever know? Our sense of who we are is determined by the stuff that fills our minds. The blow to my head – though a rock on a bank above a Scottish river was its immediate cause, its ultimate cause was the blow to my heart – emptied me of stuff. Now that I am full again, I am the stuff of which my writing is a record.

Yet as I have tried to remember, tried to write, for much of the time I have been hearing the voices, the one voice especially. They were stronger than me, he was more alive than me. My own past has, I fear, been forced out of the picture. The person I was supposed to be recovering seemed far away, whereas the voices were nearly always near.

I think that my principal fault before the blow must have been self-absorption. So perhaps it is a good thing that I have become another. A further pinprick of memory here: reading Rimbaud when I was in Paris, thrilling to his 'Je est un autre', wishing I could discuss it with Elder. If I am no longer myself, if in some sense the strongest of the voices has become me, then maybe I have felt in my blood and felt along my heart the nature of that sympathetic identification which I debated so earnestly, so abstractly, when I was a student.

Thanks to – I prefer the French here, *grâce à*, by the

grace of – the voices, I have escaped my egotism. By their infusion, *je est devenu un autre*. I do not believe in reincarnation, but I have an absolute conviction that if there is any value in this writing, that value is the tiny bit of renewed life or added immortality it may give to another William.

Whatever is placed beyond the reach of sense and knowledge, whatever is imperfectly discerned, the imagination pieces out at its leisure; and all but the present moment, but the present spot, passion claims for its own, and brooding over it with wings outspread, stamps it with an image of itself. Passion is lord of infinite space, and distant objects please because they border on its confines, and are moulded by its touch. When I was a boy, I lived within sight of a range of lofty hills, whose blue tops blending with the setting sun had often tempted my longing eyes and wandering feet. At last I put my project in execution, and on a nearer approach, instead of glimmering air woven into fantastic shapes, found them huge lumpish heaps of discoloured earth.

Distance of time has the same effect as distance of place. Time takes out the sting of pain; the instant the pressure of unwelcome circumstances is removed, the mind recoils from their hold, recovers its elasticity, and reunites itself to that image of good, which is but a reflection and configuration of its own nature. Seen in the distance, in the long perspective of waning years, the meanest incidents, enlarged and enriched by countless recollections, become interesting; the most painful, broken and softened by time, soothe. How any object, that unexpectedly brings back to us old scenes and associations, startles the mind! The drying clothes falling towards the fire.

In pretending to be what we were at a particular moment of time, we are really trying to be all that we have since been, trying to have our lives a second time around. It is in truth not the little, glimmering, almost annihilated speck in the distance that rivets our attention: it is the interval that separates us from it, and of which it is the trembling boundary, that excites our heart. Into that great gap in our being come infinite regrets. It is the contrast, the change from what we were then, that arms the half-extinguished recollection with its giant strength. In contemplating its utmost verge, we overlook the map of our existence, and re-tread, in apprehension, the journey of life.

I have learnt now to tell from the style that the voice is not mine. But I am utterly at ease with the knowledge. For I know that the thought has become mine. It does not matter whose voice it is – though I would like to know, so that I could thank the owner – because what matters is that I have discovered the truth of the words for myself. I am no longer in search of an answer to the question of whether a man is made of what he has done or what he has read.

The truth of the words is more true and more pleasing because it comes from far away. It is itself the kind of distant object for which I was pleading when I was unable to see beyond the near subject, the near pain. And now that Sarah, the subject, the pain, has herself started to fade into the distance, she is beginning to please. There is a peace in the residue of sadness with which she has left me.

But then was I not all along impelled by her aloofness?

Without it there would have been no desire. I do not think that I would have been able to keep her; I am far from sure that I would have wanted to do so. It was her elusiveness which kept me suspended. The necessary third thing. The length of my desire was the distance she did not allow me to go. Ah but its intensity! No one will ever be able to say that William did not know what it is to be in love. To have been in love is a grand memory to take through the rest of life. Distant objects, please.

Epilogue

It was nearly midnight when Laura got home. The phone was ringing. Amanda, of course.

'Where have you *been*? I've been trying all night.'

Laura explained in as few words as possible.

Amanda then informed her that the essay about the fight had been written by William Hazlitt, a contemporary of the Romantic poets. Hazlitt was apparently a failed painter, a failed philosopher, a political commentator of strong convictions but marginal influence, a successful theatre critic and lecturer on literature.

'What used to be called a man of letters,' Amanda continued, going into what Laura thought of as her sister's academic seminar voice. 'A position only possible in the particular conditions of the nineteenth-century literary marketplace.'

Then she gave Laura what she wanted. 'You asked about his life. He pursued young women. Uneducated women – he fell out with William Wordsworth over an incident involving a village girl in the Lake District, the details of which have never been untangled. In 1820 he became obsessed with a girl called Sarah Walker, the daughter of the keeper of his lodgings in Southampton Buildings in London. He divorced his wife, but then discovered that he wasn't the only lodger to be granted sexual favours by the Walker girl. He nearly had a breakdown, then he tried to purge himself of the affair by writing a confessional narrative of it, called *Liber Amoris*.'

'Called what?' asked Laura.

'Latin – the book of love. Is this something to do with your amnesiac?'

Amanda always knew. Laura evaded the question.

'Did the book do the trick?'

'That's what I asked, too. The book definitely seems to have been written to get Sarah out of his system. He took a lot of stick for publishing it. Maybe it helped, though – he remarried very quickly. Not much is known about his second wife, but Bernard – my colleague – took the view that both Hazlitt's marriages were unions of sense rather than sensibility.'

'So he didn't break the pattern?'

'Apparently not. He died five or six years later and, according to one of his friends, when he was lying on his deathbed he was agitated about financial provision for another woman he'd become obsessed with. She was described as *one of the girls of the theatre* and I don't think that meant an actress.'

'What sort of a man was he? Apart from the womanizing.'

'The sort of man who literally banged his head against the wall when he missed a stroke at racketball. Bernard stressed that he was very good at that game, though why men think that sporting prowess has anything to do with anything important is still beyond me.'

Laura would usually have risen to this. She liked to pick fights with Amanda over her attitude to men. But not now. She was kicking herself for not seeking all this information sooner. Out of some misguided idealism, she had wanted the conversations to come to their resolution without external interference.

Amanda registered her sister's desire not to talk further. 'You must be bushed and I've got a deadline on this James draft for my publisher. Let's have a proper natter towards the end of the week, when it's no longer hanging over me.'

Laura silently thanked her sister for giving her space. She put down the phone. She felt empty.

At first she could only think of herself as a dupe. Then she began to think of it as an interesting case history. Why should 'William' not be taken at his word? There was little doubt that he had initially suffered amnesia as a result of his fall. If his way of reconstructing an identity was by projection into the life of a dead writer, then so be it. Was it her role to deprive her patient of this Hazlitt character, in whom he genuinely seemed to have faith?

She had scribbled a few notes whilst she was reading his account of Sarah. Funny that she had spent so long with his writing pad in the very room in which she had previously spent time with him. As if the writing itself were on the couch.

The Monday morning team meeting was only a few hours away now. A runaway was going to be a blot on her copybook. Bill Braddock would be silently crowing. But then hadn't she been instructed to get rid of 'William' and free up a bed? Had she not planned to discharge him on Monday morning? She would have little difficulty in putting together an account of the origins of his condition.

She looked at her notes and smiled. She would tell them how valuable her writing cure had proved, how it had revealed his obsessions with death and the breast. Themes familiar to any student of Melanie Klein. In their conversations, the breakthrough had come with the discovery – or, more probably, the invention – of his baby's death. Under hypnosis, the most forceful infant memory had been the disappearance of his little sister. Confirmation had come from his two most revealing statements about Sarah, which she had copied down: 'To hold her breast was to have come home, a place I had never been with my wife', and, 'It was tenderness, not sex, for she was the daughter I never had'.

It was of no consequence how much was memory and how much was invention. Find the paradigm and then you'd see the pattern. The truth was always there in the pattern. Her guess was that a sister had been born before he was fully weaned, that he had therefore been angry at his premature deprivation of the mother's breast, then guilty when the sister died, because he had wanted her to die. All this well before the age of two.

And who was the adult 'William'? A loner, she guessed. Probably brought up as an only child after the baby sister's death. His parents would also be dead by now. He would have been unmarried, socially ill at ease, but with a love of books nurtured in his solitary youth and facilitated by a formidable memory for what he read.

So why should he not find a family for himself in his imagination?

Then she saw the point of Amanda's project, the force of her belief in the inextricability of psychologizing and story-telling. In his loneliness, 'William' needed the story about Sarah. In her own desire to make sense of things, she needed the story about his real family which she had just pieced together.

Perhaps she should write up 'The Case of *William* ?' and publish it, like Luria's history of Veniamin. If Amanda Foster was going to have her name on the front of *The Brothers James*, Laura Foster could have her name on a book too.

'What's it about, then?' people would ask.

'It's about a man with a photographic memory who gets amnesia and ends up thinking he's an obscure nineteenth-century writer called William Hazlitt.'

'And why have you written it?'

She thought long and hard about this one. Best to admit it.

'To get him out of my system. I fell in love with him, you see.'

'And has the book done the trick?'

Again, better be honest.

Not really. *Is there an art of falling out of love? No. Love is only vanquished by a succeeding love.*